Steele Empire: Raptor Squadron

Steele Empire, Volume 2

Mixon Trammell

Published by Mixon Trammell, 2024.

This is a work of fiction. Similarities to real people, places, or events are entirely coincidental.

STEELE EMPIRE: RAPTOR SQUADRON

First edition. November 5, 2024.

Copyright © 2024 Mixon Trammell.

ISBN: 979-8227175007

Written by Mixon Trammell.

Also by Mixon Trammell

Steele Empire
Steele Empire: Frontier Ranger
Steele Empire: Raptor Squadron

Dedicated to my beautiful wife. Your constant support, encouragement, and love mean more to me than you will ever know.

Preface

Looking back, I wish I had included a preface in my first book, *Frontier Ranger*, as well—but I suppose we live and learn.

Let me start by saying that while this is the second book in my *Steele Empire* series, reading the first book isn't necessary to understand this one. My vision for the *Steele Empire* series is to create a shared universe in which each story can stand on its own.

Eventually, I would love to write a crossover book, bringing characters from the individual stories together for an epic adventure—but that's a bit further down the road.

Both this book and *Frontier Ranger* were originally released as episodic content for a site that, unfortunately, no longer exists. As a result, the structure and flow of those original episodes are somewhat different from what you see in the novels. Converting them to book format required a specific process, which has influenced their final forms. The third book (which I'm still working on as I write this) will have a slightly different feel as a result.

Thank you so much for reading my book. Writing these stories brings me immense joy, and it means the world to me that you've taken time out of your busy life to explore this universe with me.

Prologue

In the latter half of the 21st century, humanity encountered the unknown: a massive wormhole appeared just outside the solar system. While global powers argued over who would control this celestial phenomenon, billionaire tech mogul Landon Steele quietly launched his own secret expeditions. But his actions drew swift opposition, and after corporate and governmental forces tried to seize his company, Steele moved his operations offshore, creating a private military with technology advanced enough to protect his vision.

Steele's team soon verified the wormhole's stability and discovered it led to an entirely different galaxy. Beyond it lay an uncharted star system and, remarkably, a habitable planet they named Gaia Prime. Driven by this discovery, Steele poured his resources into exploration, moving his entire operation through the wormhole and cutting all ties with Earth. On Gaia Prime, he founded the Steele Empire—humanity's first off-world civilization.

Two hundred years have passed. The Steele Empire has grown into a galaxy-spanning civilization with Gaia Prime as its capital. Independent and self-sufficient, the Empire no longer has any contact with Earth. Its borders are secured by a formidable Imperial Navy, constantly defending against unknown threats.

This is the story of Raptor Squadron, an elite unit of Predator-Class fighter pilots who risk everything to protect the Empire's way of life.

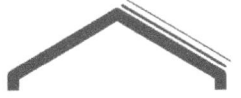

Chapter 1: Raptor Squadron

The hum of Midway Station's life-support systems reverberated through the cold metal corridors, a constant reminder of its distance from the comforts of the core worlds. Positioned at the edge of the Steele Empire's territory, Midway served as the last vestige of civilization before the wild frontier. The station wasn't just a refueling hub-it was a fortress, a defensive line holding back the chaos that threatened the Empire's expansion.

Midway Station had once been a mostly civilian-operated commercial hub until the recent war with the rogue cyborg Vanguard. During the Vanguard's advance toward the core planets, the station was evacuated, leaving it abandoned as the frontlines shifted. Now, however, Midway and many stations like it have been taken over by Imperial Military forces.

For the past several weeks, ships and personnel have arrived steadily, transforming Midway Station into a vigilant guardian over the Empire's frontier regions.

Raptor squadron had just arrived. Their mission was simple: defend Midway and keep the frontier raiders, rogue AI, and pirate gangs from pushing into the Empire's heartland. The squadron was equipped with Predator-Class starfighters, cutting-edge ships designed for speed and lethal precision. Pilots chosen for this squadron were handpicked for their skills and ability to operate under pressure.

Lieutenant Jax Ryland, the squadron leader, stood in the hanger bay, watching the engineers run diagnostics on his sleek black and silver starfighter. Jax had been on the front lines before, piloting a Shadow-Class recon fighter in the recent engagements against the Vanguard, but this new assignment felt different. The Predator was built for combat, and with recent intelligence on Wraith activity near Midway, he knew they would be put to the test soon.

The Wraiths were once a minor pirate gang, a mere annoyance along the fringes and trade routes of Imperial space. Recently, however, they were overtaken by the Vanguard, and both the size and sophistication of their fleet have grown exponentially. Following the defeat of Vanguard Prime, Wraith activity has shifted to opportunistic piracy and targeted strikes against military installations.

Jax's squadron was assembling beside him, a mix of hardened veterans and promising rookies, all eager to prove themselves.

"Welcome to Midway Station," Jax said, his voice cutting through the din of the hanger. "This isn't like the core. We're far from Imperial reinforcements, and it's our job to make sure nothing gets past this point. You've all been briefed on the Wraiths pirate gang, but we have more to worry about than just them. The Vanguard are still out there, we also have mercenaries and rogue AI to worry about—they're all threats."

Lieutenant Keira Vale, second-in-command, nodded. She had a reputation as one of the best tacticians in the fleet. "We stick to formation, watch each other's six, and we'll be fine," she added, her gaze settling on the new recruits.

Among the rookies was a young pilot named Cassian Gray. Fresh from the training academy, he had never seen real combat, but his scores in the flight simulations were off the charts. He was nervous, but determined to prove he belonged.

"Are the Vanguard still a threat?" Cassian asked, his voice betraying a hint of unease.

Jax narrowed his eyes. "If the Vanguard show up, we adapt and fight. But our priority is Midway."

"But didn't we take care of the Vanguard?" Cassian asked. "Those two Rangers did, I mean," he quickly added.

"The Rangers took out Vanguard Prime and a few others," Jax replied. "But from what I understand, there are still a couple of Vanguard units unaccounted for."

Cassian nodded, still looking uneasy. Just then, the alarm blared, cutting their conversation short.

"Unscheduled inbound ships," the voice over the station intercom announced. "All Raptor Squadron pilots to your ships."

Jax clenched his fist and turned towards his starfighter. "Looks like you'll get your chance to see action sooner than you thought," he said to Cassian.

Raptor Squadron scrambled to their fighters, engines roaring to life. The sleek arrowhead-shaped ships shot out of the station, forming up in a defensive perimeter. As they broke through the station's shielded airlock, the void of space greeted them, stars glittering against the black expanse.

Keira's voice crackled over the comm. "Multiple bogeys on approach. Fighters and frigates. Looks like Wraiths."

"Copy that," Jax replied. "Raptor Squadron, form up on me. Let's show these pirates what we're made of."

As the Wraith ships appeared on their scanners, Jax's heart raced. This was the proving ground, not just for the squadron but for the Empire's newest squadron of Predator-Class fighters. Midway was counting on them.

"Raptors, engage!"

Chapter 2: Drone Swarm

The Predator-Class fighters roared into formation, cutting through the void with silent precision. The Wraith ships, a ragtag collection of scavenged fighters and larger, more ominous frigates, were already closing in. Jax's fingers hovered over his controls, the heads-up display illuminating the cockpit with tactical readouts.

"Keira, break off with Beta wing and take the flank. Alpha with me," Jax ordered through the comms.

"Copy that, Jax," Keira replied, her voice steady.

Cassian, in Alpha wing, took a deep breath and adjusted his grip on the flight stick. His heart pounded in his chest as the first Wraith fighters appeared on his scope, darting forward like vultures. He could hear the intensity in his own voice over the comm, but he forced his hands to steady. This was it.

"Eyes on the lead fighter, Cassian," Jax's voice cut through the noise. "Stay sharp, no heroics. Cover your wingman."

Cassian's training kicked in. He tightened his formation with his wingman, Lieutenant Marko Gale, a grizzled pilot who had fought in dozens of skirmishes.

The first exchange came quick. Jax and Keira's wings split off like arrows, their ships locking on to the Wraith fighters. Green bolts of laser fire crisscrossed the battlefield, lighting up the blackness of space.

"Engaging lead frigate," Keira's calm voice announced as Beta wing swung around the Wraith formation, targeting the larger vessels.

Jax and Alpha wing sliced through the Wraith fighters, their ships moving as one. The Predator-Class starfighter was a marvel, sleek, agile, and responsive, Jax's fighter rolled, twisted, and evaded, each movement smooth and fluid, as he peppered the Wraith ship with laser fire, sending it spinning off into space.

Cassian's fighter followed close behind Gale's, keeping formation as ordered. Suddenly, two Wraith ships peeled off, targeting them with a barrage of fire.

"Stay tight, Gray!" Gale barked over the comms, dodging and weaving through the onslaught.

Cassian's fingers danced over the controls, pulling the predator into a tight barrel roll, avoiding the first salvo. The second Wraith fighter was on him in an instant, laser bolts streaming past his cockpit. Panic surged, but he fought it back, his training pushing him to act.

"I've got him," Cassian muttered to himself. His targeting system locked onto the pursuing Wraith fighter. He squeezed the trigger, and his starfighter jolted as his lasers fired. The shots found their mark, hitting the Wraith ship's engines, causing it to explode in a brief burst of fire and debris.

"Nice shot!" Gale said, impressed. "Keep your head in the game. We've got more company."

Meanwhile, Jax was weaving through a storm of laser fire, staying just ahead of the Wraith fighter on his tail. "Keira, what's your status?"

"Frigate's shields are down, targeting their main weapons," Keira responded. "We're taking heavy fire, though. They've got drone fighters inbound."

"Drones?" Jax cursed under his breath. The Wraiths were getting more advanced. These weren't their usual scavenged ships, their time as part of the Vanguard had greatly increased the threat they posed.

Suddenly, alarms blared in Jax's cockpit. A large drone swarm appeared on his HUD, headed straight for the station.

The drones were small, unmanned fighters designed to overwhelm enemy ships and defenses. Lightly armored and armed with simple laser cannons, they relied on superior numbers. Once they swarmed a target, they would crash into it, their power cores exploding and causing maximum damage.

"Raptor Squadron, we've got incoming drones heading for Midway Station," Jax called. "All wings, focus on those drones. We can't let them through!"

Cassian's heart skipped a beat as the swarm came into view, a mass of small, agile drones, their red optics glowing ominously. They moved fast, too fast.

"Marko, we have to intercept!" Cassian shouted.

"We're on it!" Gale responded, flipping his ship around.

The swarm was relentless. Raptor Squadron dove into the cloud of drones, their ships twisting and turning in complex maneuvers as they fired wildly at the approaching threat. Drones exploded one after another, but there were too many.

"They're going to break through!" Keira warned, her voice urgent.

Jax gritted his teeth, the Wraiths had planned this. While the fighters and frigates distracted the squadron, drones were targeting the station itself.

"Form a defensive line!" Jax ordered. We can't let them get to Midway."

The squadron tightened up, trying to hold the swarm at bay, but it was clear they were outnumbered. Drones buzzed past, some heading directly for the station's hull.

Just as it seemed the drones would break through, a new voice crackled over the comms.

"This is Commander Dalen of the Imperial Warship Resolute. Reinforcements inbound."

From the blackness of space, the Resolute, and Imperial Warship, burst into the fight, unleashing a barrage of missiles and laser fire that tore through the Wraith's frigates and drone swarm. Raptor Squadron's relief was palpable as the enemy ships scrambled to retreat under the new onslaught.

Jax let out a breath he didn't realize he was holding. "About time."

The drones scattered, many being wiped out by the Imperial Warships firepower. The Wraith fighters broke off, retreating into the depths of space.

Cassian, still catching his breath, leaned back in his cockpit. "Did we just survive that?"

"Don't get too comfortable," Jax said. "They'll be back, this was just the first wave. Probably testing our defenses."

As the remaining Wraith ships vanished from the scanners, Jax knew the battle for midway station was far from over.

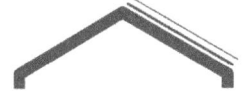

Chapter 3: A Figure In The Shadows

The dim, smoky atmosphere of the station's bar hummed with life. Pilots and crewmembers mingled, laughter and the occasional cheer echoing off the walls. Raptor Squadron had claimed a corner of the bar, their excitement still buzzing from the battle earlier that day.

Cassian sat at the center of the group; a grin plastered on his face despite the light jabs being thrown his way.

"First time in real combat and he gets a kill. Beginner's luck!" Marko Gale teased, raising his glass to the others.

Keira Vale smirked, taking a sip of her drink. "I don't know, Cassian. If that barrel roll was any tighter, you'd have corkscrewed into the Wraith ship yourself."

"Hey, it worked, didn't it?" Cassian shot back, his tone good-natured, though his cheeks flushed slightly. "I'm still here, and that Wraith is just space debris."

"That's because Gale saved your tail," One of the other pilots chimed in, triggering another round of laughter.

Cassian rolled his eyes, unable to hide his grin. "Alright, alright. I'll buy the next round of drinks. Happy?"

"Now you're talking!" Gale clapped him on the back, almost knocking him off his stool.

As the celebration continued, the squadron grew louder, drinks flowing freely. A few of the station's regulars watched from a distance, eyeing the newcomers with a mix of curiosity and indifference.

Unnoticed in the corner of the bar, a lone figure sat quietly, nursing a drink that remained mostly untouched. His dark cloak draped over his shoulders, casting deep shadows over his face. From beneath the hood, his eyes flickered across the room, watching Raptor Squadron as they reveled in their victory. He sat still, patient, blending into the dim atmosphere so well that no one seemed to notice his presence.

The figure's gaze lingered on Jax Ryland's empty chair, his brow furrowing slightly. After a long moment, he stood, moving with purpose as he slipped out of the bar, disappearing into the station's labyrinthine corridors.

MEANWHILE, IN THE QUIET of Jax's quarters, Commander Dalen sat across from Jax, both men nursing a glass of whiskey. The hum of the station was muted here, allowing a rare moment of peace amidst the tension of their duties.

Jax took a sip of his drink, studying Dalen's expression. "So, Commander, what brings the Resolute this far out?"

Dalen sat his glass down, his face grim. "Wraith activity has escalated out here. It's more than just a few raids, Jax. Intel suggests they've established a base somewhere in this sector. They've been gathering resources again, recruiting, and building up strength. The attack on Midway today? That was just a probe. They're testing our defenses."

Jax frowned, swirling the amber liquid in his glass. "I thought the Wraiths were back to just being scavengers and pirates again. Are they really that organized now that they aren't with the Vanguard?"

"They are," Dalen replied, his voice low. "There's something bigger at play. We've heard whispers of a central command structure. They obviously learned from their time with the Vanguard. It's why I'm here. Midway Station is a critical point in the Empire's Defense, and if they take it, they'll have a foothold to raid the frontier and possibly push toward the core."

Jax nodded, his mind racing. "What's out next move?"

"We're conducting patrols, but we need more intel. If the Wraiths have a base in this region, we need to find it and take it out before they can hit us again." Dalen leaned forward, his tone serious. "I need your squadron ready, this was just the beginning."

Jax clenched his jaw, knowing the weight of responsibility was growing heavier. "Raptor Squadron will be ready, Commander. You can count on us."

Dalen nodded, finishing his drink. "Good. Because if we fail out here, the entire frontier is at risk."

IN THE DEPTHS OF MIDWAY Station, the shadowy figure moved with practiced stealth, slipping into a dimly lit alley behind the bar. He checked his surroundings once before pulling a small, odd-looking communications device from inside his jacket. The device was sleek, black, with unfamiliar markings etched into its surface, definitely not of an Imperial design.

He pressed a button, and the screen blinked to life with an eerie green glow. After a moment, a voice crackled through the device.

"Report."

The figure glanced around one more time, ensuring no one was near. "I've arrived at the station. Raptor Squadron is here, just like you said. Their leader, Ryland, is meeting with the Commander of the Resolute from what I overheard the rest of the squadron saying."

"Good," the voice responded, cold and emotionless. "Everything is proceeding according to plan. The next phase will begin soon. Stay in position and await further instructions."

The figure nodded. "Understood."

The voice paused for a moment, then added, "Make sure nothing interferes with the operation."

The figure pocketed the device, a shadow passing over his face as he disappeared into the darkness of the alley. The Wraiths were already in motion, and soon, the real battle for Midway Station would begin.

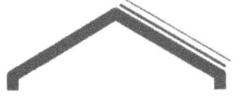

Chapter 4: Shortness Of Breath

Raptor Squadron had just completed their morning briefing when Jax announced they'd be spending the next several hours in virtual flight simulators. This was routine training, but it was crucial for honing their skills without risking lives or valuable hardware. In the simulators, they could push their limits, sharpening both reflexes and teamwork under controlled conditions that still felt painfully real.

Cassian, Jax, and the rest of the pilots strapped into their VR pods as the simulation flickered to life around them. Each pilot felt the simulated rush of acceleration as they launched into a sequence of complex combat scenarios. Enemy ships moved with the precision of real opponents, each wave more challenging than the last. Cassian gripped his controls, weaving expertly through enemy fire, while Jax coordinated with him to take down a heavily shielded bomber. The simulation tested their reflexes, tactics, and resilience, replicating the intensity of real battle, down to the sweat dripping into their eyes.

After hours of simulated dogfights, the system declared an Imperial victory. Sweaty and riding the adrenaline high, the pilots exited the pods and headed to the locker room, their chatter filled with laughter and friendly ribbing. They peeled out of their flight suits, grabbing towels and cooling off as they swapped stories about close calls in the sim. Cassian was in the middle of reenacting his final takedown when, suddenly, the door to the room sealed with a sharp hiss, halting all conversation. The lights dimmed, and a cold, mechanical voice filled the room:

"Warning. Depressurization imminent. Evacuate immediately."

The room froze as the words sank in. Panic flashed across Cassian's face as he lunged at the door, trying to force it open. Jax joined him, both of them grunting and straining to pry the door apart, but it wouldn't budge. The air thinned quickly, and the pilots began gasping for breath.

"We're locked in!" one of the pilots shouted, fear edging into their voice.

"Stay calm, work together!" Jax barked, attempting to keep everyone focused. But the harsh truth remained: they were trapped and running out of air fast.

That's when Rafe, the squadron's tech expert, whipped out his personal comm device. Gasping shallowly, he fumbled with the screen, his fingers flying over the controls as he interfaced with the station's systems. He worked with laser focus, his hands trembling from both exertion and oxygen deprivation as he attempted to bypass the security protocols that had sealed them in.

"I've got this," he managed, his voice barely a whisper as his vision started to blur. The pressure was crushing, both physically and mentally. Around him, the pilots were struggling to stay upright, their faces pale and lips blue.

Cassian fell to his knees, his world narrowing as he fought to stay conscious. Jax slumped against the wall, his breath faint. They were all on the brink of blackout when, finally, Rafe cracked the system. With a final, desperate tap, he broke through the security defenses. The door hissed and slid open, releasing a precious rush of fresh air.

The pilots stumbled out into the hallway, gasping and collapsing as they gulped down the revitalizing oxygen. Rafe, drenched in sweat and visibly shaken, leaned heavily against the wall, his comm device still clutched in his hand. They were alive—but only just.

Later, after the squadron had recovered and received clearance from the station's medical personnel, they gathered in the briefing room to debrief on the incident. Station security had already sealed off the locker room and launched an investigation, but the tension remained high. Rafe, still pale from their close call, looked at the team grimly as he shared his findings.

"The station's systems were hacked," he reported, his voice dark. "Someone accessed the control terminal in the fleet office and sealed the door remotely. This wasn't a malfunction or an accident."

Jax clenched his fists, anger flashing in his eyes. "Who the hell would try to kill us like that? And how did they even get access?"

Rafe shook his head, his expression a mix of frustration and worry. "I don't know yet. The terminal logs were wiped clean. Whoever did this knew exactly what they were doing—they left no trace."

A heavy silence blanketed the room as they absorbed the gravity of Rafe's words. Someone on Midway Station had deliberately targeted them, and the motive was unknown. But the threat was undeniably real—and unfinished business.

"Stay sharp," Jax warned, his voice steady but serious. "If they're bold enough to make a move like this, it's only a matter of time before they try again."

Chapter 5: Blind Jumps

The briefing room aboard Midway Station was tense as Raptor Squadron sat before Commander Dalen, who stood at the front with arms crossed, his expression grim. Recent events on Midway weighed heavily on everyone's minds, especially after the squadron's narrow escape from the locker room incident. Jax, Cassian, and the others were still reeling, their minds racing with unanswered questions.

"Listen up," Dalen's voice cut through the tension. "We don't have time to dwell on what happened yesterday. There's a mission that needs your full attention." He paused, letting the weight of his words sink in. "The *Resolute* is heading deep into pirate territory for a raid on a suspected Wraith base, which means we won't be available for our normal escort duties for ships traveling to and from Midway. Raptor Squadron will jump to Archibald Station to meet a civilian supply fleet and escort them back here. Ensure their safe arrival."

Jax leaned forward, his brow furrowed. "What kind of resistance are we expecting, sir?"

Dalen shrugged slightly. "Standard protocol. We don't foresee any resistance, but with the uptick in Wraith activity in this sector lately, anything's possible. Stay sharp."

The squad exchanged glances, nodding in silent agreement. Escort missions weren't glamorous, but they were vital to keeping Midway Station supplied and operational. After a final nod from Commander Dalen, the squadron was dismissed, and the pilots set off to prepare for the next day's mission.

Raptor Squadron departed Midway Station on schedule, their fighters flashing into lightspeed as they made their way to the rendezvous point near Archibald Station. Cassian felt the familiar pull of the jump, watching as stars stretched into bright streaks of light around him. Despite recent events, he was confident in the mission—routine escort, no anticipated threats.

Yet when they exited lightspeed, something was wrong.

"Uh, Jax?" Rafe's voice crackled over the comms. "We're... not where we're supposed to be. Like, not even remotely close."

Jax cursed under his breath. "Confirm coordinates, Rafe."

"I'm checking," Rafe replied, his tone tense. "We should have exited just outside of Archibald's defenses, but we're way off course. It's like someone at Midway fed us the wrong data."

Cassian's hands tightened on his controls. "Can we jump again to correct it?"

"Stand by." Rafe keyed in a new set of coordinates based on their briefing, and the squadron initiated a second jump. But once again, they exited at a random, unknown location, drifting in the emptiness of deep space.

"Damn it!" Rafe's frustration was clear. "The coordinates aren't working. Our jump computers have been corrupted. No matter what I input, we're being thrown to random locations."

Jax's voice was controlled but urgent. "Can you fix it?"

Rafe let out a shaky breath. "I'm trying. If I can restore my nav system, we can slave the other birds to it and jump together. But I need time."

Before anyone could respond, alarms blared in Cassian's cockpit.

"I've got multiple contacts!" he shouted. "Wraith ships incoming—a gunship, some frigates, and fighters!"

Jax muttered a curse. "Rafe, keep working. Everyone else, form up and engage!"

Cassian's heart pounded as he angled his fighter toward the incoming Wraith ships. The odds were against them; with their jump systems compromised, they couldn't escape. All they could do was fight and buy Rafe the time he needed to get them to Archibald Station.

Laser fire lit up the void as Raptor Squadron clashed with the Wraith fighters. Jax's voice was steady, barking orders as he coordinated their formation, keeping them tightly together as they maneuvered through enemy fire. The Wraith gunship loomed ominously in Cassian's viewport, its massive cannons blazing, spewing deadly trails of laser fire.

Cassian's mind raced. The gunship was a major threat, but it was slow, especially compared to his fighter. If they could neutralize it, the enemy's heavy firepower would be cut significantly.

"Cassian, stay in formation!" Jax ordered over the comm, his tone sharp.

But Cassian had other plans. A risky one. He veered away from the squadron, angling his fighter straight toward the gunship.

"Cassian, don't you dare!" Jax's voice rang out, but it was too late.

Pushing his fighter to its limits, Cassian accelerated toward the gunship, weaving through its laser fire as he closed the distance. At the last moment, he banked hard, skimming just below the gunship's hull and lining up his sights with the exposed landing bay where enemy fighters were stationed. With a quick breath, he unleashed a barrage of missiles and laser fire into the weakly shielded bay, pulling up just in time.

His shots hit home, sparking a chain reaction that detonated something critical inside. The gunship lurched, flames erupting from its landing bay before it spiraled out of control and exploded.

Cassian exhaled, his heart racing. He knew he'd pay for breaking formation, but the gunship was down.

"I told you not to pull that stunt, Cassian!" Jax's growl came through the comm, tinged with frustration. "You could have gotten yourself killed."

"Yeah," Cassian replied, trying to mask his nervousness, "but it worked."

The Wraith fighters regrouped, preparing for a second assault, when Rafe's voice cut through the comms. "I've got it! Nav system's online. Slave your computers to mine—now!"

With no time to waste, the squadron quickly formed up around Rafe's fighter, linking their systems. Jax gave the order, and in a flash, they jumped, leaving the Wraith task force behind.

When Raptor Squadron came out of lightspeed this time, they were exactly where they were supposed to be. Archibald Station loomed before them, and the civilian supply fleet awaited. Relief swept through the squadron as they formed up around the slow-moving supply vessels, ready to escort them safely back to Midway Station.

Inside his cockpit, Jax couldn't shake a lingering sense of unease. First, someone had tried to kill them in the locker room; now, their jump computers had been sabotaged. It was too much to dismiss as coincidence. Someone on Midway Station was targeting his squadron, but why?

As the stars stretched into streaks on their journey back to Midway, Jax mulled over the implications, realizing that whatever game their unseen enemy was playing, it was far from over.

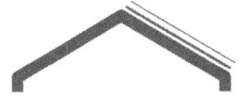

Chapter 6: Two Man Escort

Raptor Squadron returned to Midway Station, guiding the civilian supply fleet through the asteroid-laden approach with practiced precision. As they neared their docking bays, a new arrival caught their attention: the *SSV Providence*, a massive carrier warship, was docked with one of the station's exterior rings. The *Providence* housed several squadrons of Predator-Class fighters, Shadow-Class recon ships, and the imposing Mauler-Class bombers—a formidable display of Imperial strength.

Cassian, eyeing the carrier from his cockpit, couldn't help but admire its sleek, deadly design. "Just what we needed," he muttered to Jax with a hint of sarcasm, "more brass around to tell us how to do our job."

Jax chuckled. "Gotta love the support, right?"

Later, as Raptor Squadron made their way to the station's bar to unwind, they found it packed with crew members and pilots from the *Providence*. The atmosphere was lively, but the air bristled with an unspoken tension as Jax led his team inside. The pilots from the *Providence*, dressed in crisp uniforms, regarded the station-based squadron with barely concealed superiority, as if looking down on those who patrolled the fringe rather than serving on the "real" frontlines.

Cassian felt a pair of eyes on him as he walked past the bar counter. A Mauler pilot, a tall, broad-shouldered man with a confident smirk, blocked his path. "You guys still running out of this dusty old outpost?" he sneered. "No wonder you haven't earned a spot on a real warship yet."

Cassian, weary from the long escort mission, fixed him with a sharp look. "We handle our business just fine out here. Not all of us need a flying fortress to feel important."

The words hung in the air, and tension flared instantly. A few more taunts were exchanged, sharp and biting, until the Mauler pilot gave Cassian a rough shove. Cassian's patience snapped—he cocked back his fist and drove it squarely into the pilot's nose.

The bar erupted into chaos. Raptor and *Providence* pilots jumped in, turning the confrontation into a full-blown brawl. Bottles shattered, tables overturned, and laughter quickly turned to shouts of anger as fists flew. The pilots from both squadrons grappled and swung, venting frustrations and proving their toughness, each side unwilling to back down.

Station security stormed in, fighting through the mass of tangled pilots to pull them apart. Cassian, bloody but defiant, was dragged off alongside the bomber pilot he'd hit. Both were taken to the brig, accompanied by several other bruised and battered pilots from each squadron.

Inside the brig, tensions remained thick. Cassian and the bomber pilot—Lieutenant Neal, as he'd learned—glared at each other from across their shared cell.

"Station jockey couldn't handle a little teasing," Neal sneered, his tone mocking.

Cassian shot back, "You're lucky they broke us up when they did, fleet boy."

The argument was on the verge of reigniting when Commander Dalen and Captain Valon of the *Providence* stormed into the brig, their faces dark with anger.

"Enough!" Dalen's voice boomed, silencing the room. He cast a disappointed glare at Cassian, then at Neal. "Do you two know how childish this looks? You're supposed to be elite pilots, not barroom brawlers."

Captain Valon nodded sharply. "You're all on the same side, and I will not tolerate this behavior. You two," he pointed directly at Cassian and Neal, "are going to learn to work together—starting now."

Cassian frowned, puzzled. "What do you mean, sir?"

"You and Lieutenant Neal here," Dalen replied, gesturing toward Neal, "will be escorting the civilian supply fleet back to Archibald Station. Just the two of you."

Both men balked. "A fighter and a bomber for an entire fleet? That's suicide if we're attacked by Wraiths!" Neal protested.

"I don't care if you don't like it," Valon said sternly. "You're going to learn some respect for each other, and you'll start by working as a team. You leave in two hours. Dismissed."

Grumbling but knowing resistance was pointless, Cassian and Neal were released from the brig. Hours later, they launched from Midway Station alongside the civilian fleet. The journey was uneventful at first; the two pilots barely spoke, each focused on their console, maintaining a distanced formation.

As they neared Archibald Station, an alert blared across their consoles. An unknown freighter had come out of a jump directly ahead of them, and it was anything but ordinary. Bristling with weapons and armored to an unusual degree, it wasted no time in opening fire, setting its sights on the vulnerable supply ships.

"Looks like we've got company," Neal muttered, tension in his voice.

"Perfect," Cassian grimaced. "Just what we needed."

The freighter unleashed a relentless barrage, its unexpected firepower forcing Cassian and Neal to dive and weave, dodging the deadly onslaught as they returned fire. Cassian's fighter lasers did little against the freighter's heavy shielding, but he kept at it, trying to draw its attention away from the civilian ships.

"This thing's packing way more than I expected!" Cassian shouted as a volley narrowly missed his wing.

"Keep him busy—I'll focus on the engines, see if we can slow him down," Neal replied, his voice all business.

Forgetting their earlier tension, the two began working in sync. Cassian made daring strafing runs to draw the freighter's fire, while Neal used the Mauler's heavier armaments to target the freighter's engines. The two pilots coordinated their movements, each covering the other, pressing hard against the freighter's defenses until its shields began to flicker.

Cassian saw his chance. "Almost got it! Keep the pressure on!"

Finally, with a direct hit to its rear, one of the freighter's engines exploded. Realizing it was outmatched, the freighter veered off, activating its jump drive to escape the system as quickly as it had arrived.

Breathing heavily, Cassian watched it disappear, a wave of relief washing over him. He glanced over at Neal's cockpit through his viewport, and the two shared a weary but satisfied nod as they regrouped with the fleet.

On the return trip to Midway, the tension between the two pilots had thawed considerably. "That freighter was a serious piece of work," Cassian remarked, breaking the silence.

"Yeah," Neal agreed. "Not your usual pirate setup. Someone with deep pockets outfitted that thing."

As they landed back at Midway, Commander Dalen and Captain Valon awaited them. Dalen raised an eyebrow as the two climbed out of their cockpits.

"Glad to see you two didn't kill each other," Dalen remarked dryly.

Cassian and Neal exchanged grins, a camaraderie born from the heat of battle. "No, sir," Neal replied. "I think we figured it out."

Valon allowed himself a slight smile. "Good. You'll need that teamwork out here on the frontier."

With that, Dalen dismissed them, but the encounter left Cassian with an unsettled feeling. Whoever had sent that armed freighter wasn't an ordinary pirate. And if they were targeting supply lines, it might only be the beginning of a larger threat to Midway.

Chapter 7: Breakfast Interrupted

As Raptor Squadron gathered for their usual breakfast in the station's mess hall, the air buzzed with light banter and the clinking of trays. But beneath the surface, tension simmered. The *Providence* had left on a patrol mission, and the *Resolute* was handling a border dispute in another system, leaving Midway Station with noticeably fewer defenses. The pilots were keenly aware that their once-secure outpost had become far more vulnerable.

Jax was in the middle of a sarcastic remark about station food when a security officer appeared at the table, drawing everyone's attention. "Lieutenant Jax," the officer said, "you have an urgent call in the comm center. High priority."

Jax frowned, puzzled. "Wonder what that's about," he muttered, standing and heading for the comm center. His squad exchanged curious glances, each speculating on the nature of the call.

"Maybe it's fleet business?" Cassian suggested. "Lots of action in this sector lately."

"Could be serious," another pilot added. "Maybe the Wraiths are up to something."

When Jax returned, his expression was tense, confirming their suspicions. He sat, looking around at his squadron. "That was fleet intelligence. They've picked up intel about a major Wraith force heading toward the station."

A heavy silence fell over the table, the weight of the news sinking in.

"When?" Cassian asked, setting his fork down.

"Soon. Very soon." Jax's voice was steady but urgent. "We need to scramble our fighters. Now."

Without a second's hesitation, Raptor Squadron sprang up, racing through the corridors toward the hangar. Alarms began blaring across the station as they reached the hangar, quickly donning flight suits and prepping their ships. Just as they launched, the dreaded moment arrived.

A massive Wraith vessel jumped into the system—a ship unlike anything they had ever seen. Its sleek, ominous form was bristling with unknown weaponry and high-tech modifications, and it hovered just outside the range of Midway's defense batteries. Instead of advancing on the station, the vessel began releasing waves of drone fighters into space, each one sleek and menacing, with a faint blue glow around their fuselage. Then, as suddenly as it had arrived, the large Wraith ship jumped away, leaving its swarm of drones to face Raptor Squadron alone.

"Raptor Squadron, engage!" Jax's voice boomed over the comms, and the pilots surged forward, meeting the drones head-on. Space erupted in a maelstrom of laser fire as the squadron dove into the fray, expertly dodging and weaving through the relentless onslaught of drones.

"Watch your six!" Jax called out as Cassian narrowly avoided a drone's strafing run, the glowing energy blasts streaking past his canopy.

Cassian twisted his fighter sharply, his reflexes on high alert as he fired back, his shots hitting one of the drones dead-on and causing it to explode in a flash of light. But more drones took its place, surrounding the squadron with precision and seemingly limitless numbers. The battle raged, Raptor Squadron pushing themselves to their limits, each pilot determined to keep the drones from reaching Midway.

After several minutes, Cassian noticed something strange. "They're not targeting the station," he muttered into the comms. "They're focused solely on us."

"They're testing us," Jax realized, the grim tone in his voice audible even over the comms.

The squad fought back harder, but one by one, their fighters began taking disabling hits. Cassian's shields flickered, and a drone swooped in close, hitting his engine. Sparks flew across his controls as his ship jerked violently, his engine sputtering out.

"Dammit! My engines are down!" Cassian shouted, struggling to stabilize his drifting fighter.

"Same here," came Jax's voice, strained with frustration. "They're picking us apart, targeting critical systems!"

Despite their best efforts, the drones were overwhelming them. Raptor Squadron found themselves drifting, their ships disabled and powerless. The drones circled for a moment longer, as if evaluating their victory, before withdrawing. Moments later, the mysterious Wraith vessel reappeared, swiftly recovering the drones one by one before jumping out of the system.

"Well, this is humiliating," one of the pilots muttered over the comms, his voice thick with bitterness.

"We need to figure out how to get back to the station," Jax said, though he knew their options were limited. "We're sitting ducks out here."

Just then, their proximity sensors flared, and relief washed over the squadron as an Imperial warship, the *SSV Bellator*, jumped into the system and began moving toward their position. With practiced efficiency, the *Bellator*'s crew deployed recovery shuttles, hauling each of the disabled fighters back to Midway Station.

Back on Midway, Raptor Squadron assembled in the briefing room, still rattled from the encounter. Moments later, the commander of the *Bellator*, a tall, imposing man with a sharp gaze, entered the room. His presence alone was enough to silence the murmurs among the pilots.

"You all did well to survive that," the commander began, his voice calm but serious. "But make no mistake, this was never about defeating you."

Jax leaned forward, his eyes narrowing. "What do you mean, sir?"

The commander's expression was grim. "The Wraiths didn't send that swarm to destroy Midway or even to disable your fighters directly. They sent it to learn."

"Learn?" Cassian repeated, his voice incredulous. "Are you saying they're studying us?"

"Precisely," the commander confirmed with a nod. "We've been tracking this behavior for some time now. The Wraiths are using an advanced AI to control their drones. Today's attack wasn't about a full-scale assault; it was about analyzing your squadron's tactics, flight patterns, and weak points."

A sense of unease settled over the room as the implications sank in.

"They now have a detailed profile on Raptor Squadron," the commander continued. "The next time they engage, they'll use that data to take you down faster and more efficiently."

Cassian clenched his fists, frustration evident in his expression. "So what do we do, sir? Just wait for them to exploit everything they've learned?"

The commander shook his head, a determined glint in his eye. "No. We adapt. This AI is growing at an exponential rate, and if it's not stopped, it could become an even greater threat than a few drone swarms. Our mission is to track down its source and destroy it before it becomes unstoppable."

Jax stood, turning to address his squadron. "We're not backing down. We'll develop new strategies, new formations, whatever it takes. They might think they know us now, but we're just getting started."

The pilots exchanged grim nods, their resolve solidifying. The Wraiths had underestimated them once, but the next encounter would be different.

As the pilots filed out, Cassian caught Jax's eye. "Looks like things are heating up."

Jax nodded. "And we'd better be ready for whatever comes next."

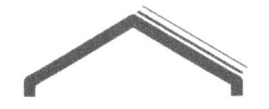

Chapter 8: No Loose Ends

In the station gym, the metallic clang of weights hitting racks echoed off the walls as Rafe and Cassian powered through their sets. The brightly lit, sterile room seemed oddly out of place for the tension brewing between the two Raptor Squadron members. Both had been replaying the strange events of recent weeks—the sabotage, the corrupted jump computers, and the drones that seemed hellbent on targeting them.

Rafe set down his barbell, wiping sweat from his brow, his expression more intense than usual. "Cass, I've been thinking," he began, his voice low. "About the locker room incident... and the jump computers getting fried."

Cassian paused mid-set, wiping down his hands. "What do you mean?"

"What if it's all connected?" Rafe glanced around the gym, ensuring no one was within earshot. "Look, that rogue AI Imperial Intelligence mentioned... What if it's behind the sabotage too? This isn't just random bad luck targeting us. It's calculated."

Cassian's brow furrowed. "You're saying you think this AI is specifically targeting Raptor Squadron?"

Rafe nodded grimly. "Exactly. I haven't told anyone yet; I've only got theories, and if I start making accusations without proof, it could lead to panic or worse—draw the wrong kind of attention."

Cassian stood, muscles taut with tension. "You need to tell Jax and Commander Dalen. If you're right, they need to know. We're already in deep, and if we're being targeted, we can't afford to sit on this."

After a moment's hesitation, Rafe finally nodded. "Alright. You're right. Let's go."

In Commander Dalen's office, the atmosphere grew heavier. Dalen sat behind his desk, a holographic sector map flickering beside him. Jax stood near the door, arms crossed, listening as Rafe laid out his theory.

When Rafe finished, Dalen leaned back, expression unreadable. "If you're right, Rafe, this is more serious than we thought. I'll make sure Imperial Intelligence gets this information. In the meantime, keep your heads down. Stay vigilant, and don't share this with anyone else. We can't risk tipping off whoever might be behind this."

Jax uncrossed his arms and gave them a grave nod. "Good work bringing this forward. But until we know for sure, assume we're being watched."

Elsewhere on the station, Lieutenant Kiera Vale jogged her usual circuit in the habitat ring, the soft hum of the artificial gravity systems accompanying her steady pace. The rhythmic thud of her feet on the metal floor was the only sound as she moved through the wide, curved corridors. Sweat beaded on her forehead, but the exercise kept her sharp, her mind clear—a comforting contrast to the recent tension gripping Midway Station.

As she neared a secluded section of the habitat ring, where the corridor narrowed near the climate control units, she slowed to catch her breath. She leaned against the railing, gazing through the observation window at the distant, tranquil stars—a stark contrast to the escalating danger surrounding Raptor Squadron.

But Kiera wasn't alone.

From the shadows between two maintenance access points, a figure emerged with eerie silence, cloaked in dark, nondescript clothing that blended perfectly with the dim lighting. His movements were precise, his approach calculated. Kiera didn't notice him until it was too late.

In one swift, practiced motion, the figure clamped a hand over her mouth, silencing her startled gasp. Before she could struggle, he pressed a small injector to her neck—a faint prick and brief hiss were all she felt before her body froze. Her vision blurred, and within seconds, she slumped against him, breath shallow, body limp.

The figure held her steady, verifying her demise before glancing around. Satisfied that no one had seen, he dragged her body behind the bulky climate control units—a perfect hiding spot, out of view and far from foot traffic. She wouldn't be discovered until long after he'd gone.

Moving swiftly, he retreated into the shadows, pulling out a sleek, unusual-looking comm device. He pressed a button, and a voice crackled on the other end.

"It's done," he reported coldly. "The first target has been eliminated."

A moment passed before the voice responded, satisfied. "Good. Proceed with the others. No loose ends."

The shadowy figure pocketed the comm and vanished into the station's unseen corners, his next target already in sight.

Chapter 9: Funeral For A Friend

The members of Raptor Squadron gathered in the massive, dimly lit hangar bay of the *Resolute* for Lieutenant Kiera Vale's funeral. The entire bay had been cleared, and rows of officers and crew, each in formal dress uniform, stood shoulder to shoulder in silent respect. The somber atmosphere was heavy, and only the soft hum of the ship's engines broke the silence. Before them lay Kiera's gleaming black coffin, draped with the Imperial Navy's flag, its dark fabric catching the faint light from the overhead fixtures. The silence felt as vast as space itself.

Commander Dalen stood at the front, his usually impassive face drawn tight with grief and responsibility. His voice, clear yet tinged with sorrow, carried across the hangar as he began the eulogy.

"Kiera Vale was more than just a pilot in Raptor Squadron," he said, each word precise and measured. "She was a protector, a warrior, and a friend. Her service to the Empire was exemplary, marked by her dedication to defending the frontiers and her unwavering commitment to her squadron." He paused, letting the weight of his words settle over the assembly.

Dalen's gaze swept across the room, the pain in his eyes just visible as he continued, "Kiera's piloting skills were unmatched. In her time with us, she became a pillar of strength, forging bonds that ran deeper than any of us could have expected. She wasn't just a member of this squadron; she was family. And family looks out for each other, always."

Dalen took a deep breath, steadying himself before he spoke again. "It is believed Kiera suffered a heart attack during her morning run—a tragic, sudden end to a life filled with promise and dedication. We mourn her passing today, but we also honor what she gave to the Empire and to each of us. She will be missed, but she will never be forgotten."

At a nod from Dalen, the honor guard approached the coffin, lifting it with solemn precision. The squadron and assembled crew stood at attention, hands raised in a final salute as the honor guard moved toward the airlock. The hangar doors opened, and as the coffin drifted into the void, the silence of the vast star-studded space swallowed Kiera's resting place, a solemn reminder of the dangers they faced every day. The squadron remained in formation, each member silently paying their respects, etched faces reflecting their individual grief.

The bar on Midway Station was dimly lit, its familiar shadows a comforting contrast to the sterile brightness of the hangar earlier. Raptor Squadron gathered around a large, circular table, drinks in hand as they attempted to find solace in shared memories. Glasses clinked occasionally, and voices were low but warm as they shared stories of Kiera's courage and quick wit. The atmosphere was a bittersweet blend of laughter through lingering sadness, and despite the loss, the squadron seemed momentarily united.

Jax nudged Rafe, chuckling, "Remember that time she scared the hell out of those rookies with that insane barrel roll? Nearly had them ejecting in the middle of a practice drill."

Rafe laughed, shaking his head. "She had them thinking they were under attack! Classic Kiera. She always knew how to keep us on our toes."

The laughter faded, replaced by a quiet, reflective mood. Jax glanced across the table, where Cassian sat apart from the others, his fists clenched around his drink, gaze fixed intensely on the glass. His expression was dark, his jaw tight, as if restraining himself from saying something he knew would change the tone.

Noticing, Jax leaned in. "Hey, Cassian," he said softly, his tone gentle. "You alright?"

Cassian's grip on the glass tightened, and he slammed it down, drawing the squadron's attention. His voice, low and edged with frustration, cut through the room's quiet. "You're all fools if you think Kiera just dropped dead from a heart attack."

The air around the table stilled, eyes turning to him in tense surprise. "What are you talking about?" Rafe asked, frowning, the usual camaraderie giving way to unease.

Cassian's gaze swept across the squadron, his eyes filled with barely contained anger. "After everything we've been through the past few weeks—the

Wraiths, the AI attacks, all the sabotage—and now this? It's all too convenient. Too damn neat. Kiera didn't just die."

Marko Gale looked over, his face darkening. "What exactly are you saying, Cassian?"

"I'm saying it wasn't natural," Cassian replied, his tone dropping even lower. "I don't know if it was the Wraiths or something else, but they wanted her gone. And we're next."

Rafe shook his head, shifting uncomfortably. "The autopsy was thorough, Cass. There was nothing suspicious. It's tragic, but things like this do happen."

Cassian stood abruptly, his chair scraping against the floor as he shot Rafe a hard look. "You don't get it. None of you do. Think about what we're up against. The Wraiths, that rogue AI—it's learning us, testing us. This wasn't an accident. Kiera was targeted." He turned his gaze to Jax, his eyes dark and determined. "Tell me you haven't thought the same thing."

Jax hesitated, glancing down at his drink before meeting Cassian's intense gaze. "I won't lie—I've been worried. This whole thing doesn't sit right with me either. But without proof..."

Marko leaned forward, his voice quiet but serious. "So what do we do about it? Sit here and wait to be picked off?"

Jax nodded, his mind already turning. "We need to keep a low profile and dig deeper, but not here. We'll be watched closely on the station. I'll talk to Commander Dalen, see if he can get us on a patrol with the *Resolute* when they head out again. We'll have more freedom to investigate. Pack your bags and be ready."

Each member nodded in agreement, a silent understanding passing among them. The lighthearted memories of Kiera had faded, replaced by a new, tense purpose. They would not let her death go unanswered.

In a small, dimly lit room with cold, metallic walls, the shadowy figure responsible for Kiera's death sat alone, expression unreadable as he watched the security feed on the terminal before him. The display showed Raptor Squadron in the station bar, their faces shadowed and solemn, their words muted but their expressions speaking volumes. The hint of satisfaction flickered in his eyes as he watched Cassian, who was clearly beginning to suspect the truth.

Reaching for a sleek, unfamiliar comm device, he pressed a button, activating the secure line. A voice, cold and mechanical, crackled from the other end.

"They're planning to leave on patrol with the *Resolute*," the figure reported, voice even and devoid of emotion.

"Good," replied the voice on the other end. "Obtain their flight plan. We'll ensure Raptor Squadron is dealt with—completely."

The line went dead with a faint click, and the figure leaned back, letting a slow, satisfied smile spread across his face. The pieces were in place. Soon, the Empire's so-called elite would realize they were not the hunters but the hunted.

Chapter 10: New Caliburn

Raptor Squadron had been stationed aboard the *Resolute* for several days, patrolling the outer edges of Wraith-occupied space. With each passing day free from conflict, the squadron channeled their energy into intensive training exercises. Maneuvering through asteroid fields and performing atmospheric flights over uninhabited planets offered both a challenge and a distraction, letting the pilots focus on honing their skills rather than on the recent loss of Kiera Vale.

Jax noticed a shift within the team. The tension that had marked their faces was gradually easing, replaced by a renewed sense of purpose. The squadron was reclaiming its old rhythm, and Jax felt a glimmer of relief. Yet, the quiet bothered him. Something about this absence of threats seemed ominous—a calm before the storm, he kept thinking.

One morning, as the squadron was preparing for a training mission, Jax led the team toward the hangar, helmets tucked under their arms. Cassian walked beside him, his silence softened since Kiera's passing, no longer carrying the same edge. The squadron exchanged jokes, the mood lighter as they neared their fighters.

Suddenly, a sharp buzz sounded over their comms. "Raptor Squadron, report to the briefing room immediately."

Jax exchanged a glance with Rafe, who shrugged. "Looks like we're off training duty."

Changing course, they made their way to the briefing room. Inside, Commander Dalen stood at the front, his usual calm replaced by a gravity that immediately drew their attention. Behind him, the holo-display showed a distant planet, its surface speckled with settlement lights.

"Take your seats," Dalen instructed, gesturing to the chairs.

Once everyone was seated, Dalen crossed his arms, his gaze solemn. "We've received a distress call from one of our frontier planets, New Caliburn. It's a small, sparsely populated world, but strategically critical to the Empire. The local garrison has been overrun by an unknown force, and they're requesting immediate assistance."

Jax leaned forward, curiosity and concern in his eyes. "Unknown force? Do we think it's the Wraiths?"

Dalen nodded, his face grim. "That's our leading theory, but the situation is complicated. The attack happened fast, and details are sketchy. New Caliburn's communications are spotty, but preliminary reports mention highly advanced drones among the attackers."

Cassian's expression darkened at the mention of drones. "Wraith AI?"

"It's possible," Dalen replied. "Imperial Intelligence believes this could be the work of the Wraiths' AI growing more aggressive. If that's true, this could be the beginning of a larger offensive targeting the frontier."

Jax glanced around, seeing the tension resurface in his squadron's faces. His mind drifted briefly to Kiera. "What's our mission, Commander?"

Dalen stepped closer to the holo-display, zooming in on New Caliburn's terrain. "We're heading there at full speed. The *Resolute* will engage the enemy in orbit, but Raptor Squadron will be deployed to the planet's surface to support the local defenses. Your primary objectives are to protect civilian populations, provide air support, and help hold the line until reinforcements arrive."

Marko Gale spoke up from the back of the room, a serious look in his eyes. "What kind of resistance are we looking at down there?"

Dalen's face hardened. "Heavy resistance. The enemy seems to have entrenched themselves in strategic locations around the settlements. This isn't a training exercise, and these drones—if they're what we suspect—will be fast, adaptive, and deadly. They've been learning."

Jax stood, his voice steady. "We're ready, sir."

Dalen gave a short nod. "Good. You launch in one hour. Prep your fighters, check your gear, and arm yourselves to the teeth. I expect nothing less than your best out there. Dismissed."

As the squadron filed out, a heavy silence settled over them. Jax walked alongside Cassian, noticing his clenched fists and the determined look in his eyes.

"You good, Cass?" Jax asked quietly.

Cassian's jaw tightened as he glanced at Jax. "It feels like we're stepping into something bigger than we realize. First Kiera, now this AI threat... It's all connected somehow. I can feel it."

Jax placed a reassuring hand on Cassian's shoulder, his voice steady. "We'll get through this. We've got each other's backs. Focus on the mission; we'll sort out the rest after."

Cassian gave a short nod, though uncertainty flickered in his eyes. Jax understood; he felt it, too.

An hour later, Raptor Squadron launched from the *Resolute*, their fighters streaking into the cold void. Ahead, New Caliburn loomed large, its surface marked with smoke and fire as the battle raged below.

Jax's voice crackled over the comms. "Alright, Raptors. Let's show them what we're made of. Stay tight, watch your six, and remember, the civilians are counting on us."

As they cut through space toward New Caliburn, red blips appeared on their HUDs, signaling multiple hostile ships closing in. Enemy forces included drones and manned Wraith fighters, all bearing down with ruthless speed.

"Alright, Raptors, we've got company," Jax called out. "Break formation and engage. Keep it tight—we can't afford to get split up out here."

The squadron shifted seamlessly, their training kicking in as they dove into combat. Their Predator-class fighters weaved through enemy fire, evading the fast, aggressive maneuvers of the Wraith fighters. But Raptor Squadron was faster.

Leading the charge, Jax banked hard to dodge a volley of laser fire, locking onto an enemy fighter. His fingers moved over the controls, releasing a pair of missiles that struck their target dead-on. The Wraith ship exploded, debris scattering into the vacuum.

"One down," Jax muttered. "Let's keep moving."

Cassian flew close behind, dodging a swarm of drones that had locked onto him. "These drones are smarter than before," he growled. "They're adapting to our moves."

"I see it," Rafe replied, firing at two drones tailing Cassian. The drones veered, but Rafe's shots clipped one, sending it spiraling out of control.

Marko dove through a debris field, taking out two Wraith ships with pinpoint shots. "Almost too easy," he joked, though tension edged his voice.

Suddenly, alarms blared across their HUDs as multiple missiles locked onto Jax. He swerved hard, narrowly evading the first, but the second missile held tight. Sweat trickled down his face as he pushed his fighter to its limits.

"Rafe, little help?" Jax called out.

"On it!" Rafe's ship swooped in, firing a well-placed shot that detonated the missile just before it reached Jax.

"Thanks. Let's finish this," Jax said, regaining control and leading the squadron in a final push. One by one, they dismantled the enemy ships and drones, clearing a path to the planet's surface.

"Good work, Raptors. We've got an opening. Let's hit the ground," Jax ordered.

The squadron formed up, descending toward New Caliburn as the atmosphere streaked across their cockpits. Below, chaos reigned, with burning Imperial outposts, thick smoke, and laser fire crisscrossing the skies. The enemy had fortified positions around the settlements, while civilians evacuated under heavy fire.

"Alright, split up," Jax commanded. "Cover as much ground as possible. Protect the civilians and take out fortified positions. We're the last line of defense."

The squadron broke off, each pilot targeting a hotspot. Jax and Cassian moved toward the largest settlement, skimming low over the ground to dodge anti-aircraft fire. Jax locked onto an artillery unit, his pulse lasers reducing the enemy vehicles to debris.

Cassian followed, strafing ground forces advancing on the evac zone. His lasers tore through Wraith ranks, buying the civilians time to board transports.

"Nice work, Cassian," Jax commended as evac ships lifted off. "Let's finish this up."

Elsewhere, Marko and Rafe covered other zones, neutralizing enemy positions. Marko, ever the risk-taker, dodged anti-aircraft rounds, sending missiles into Wraith strongholds with precision. Rafe provided cover for an Imperial outpost, decimating enemy tanks as they tried breaching the walls.

Hours passed as the squadron fought tirelessly, gradually turning the tide. The Wraith forces, outmaneuvered and off-guard, began to retreat. With one final push, the civilians were evacuated, and enemy positions lay in ruins.

Jax's voice came over the comms, triumphant. "That's it. We've done it. Ground forces are retreating, and the evac is complete."

A collective sigh of relief came over the comms. "About time we caught a break," Marko joked.

But their comms flared again, this time with Commander Dalen's urgent voice. "Raptor Squadron, return to orbit immediately. The *Resolute* is under heavy attack. We need you, now."

Jax's stomach dropped as he looked to the stars. "Copy that, Commander. We're on our way."

Ascending back into space, the squadron entered a far worse battle than anticipated. The *Resolute* was surrounded by enemy ships and drones, its hull scarred, shields flickering as it struggled to hold position.

"Damn," Rafe muttered. "This isn't good."

Jax's voice hardened. "No, it's not. But we've got a job to do. Let's even the odds."

Raptor Squadron dove into the fray, weapons blazing as they cut through enemy ranks. But the Wraiths fought fiercely, their drones moving with terrifying precision. Jax couldn't help but feel a gnawing sense of dread. This battle was far from over, and the enemy was far more dangerous than they had ever anticipated.

Chapter 11: Resolute No More

The battle around the *Resolute* had reached a fever pitch. Raptor Squadron weaved and darted through the chaos, but the situation was deteriorating fast. Waves of Wraith drones, manned fighters, and looming capital ships surged forward with relentless coordination, their attacks precise and unyielding. The *Resolute,* once a symbol of Imperial might, now drifted battered and burning, its turbolasers blazing desperately as it tried to fend off the overwhelming assault.

Jax's voice cut through the comms, urgent yet steady. "Stay tight, Raptors. Focus on the drones—they're the real threat. Keep them off the *Resolute* as long as you can."

Obeying his command, the squadron dove into the swarm, lasers and missiles streaking through the darkness as they targeted the aggressive drones. Explosions lit up the void around them, debris from destroyed fighters spinning in every direction. Cassian peeled off to target a group of drones converging on the *Resolute's* vulnerable engines, managing to destroy two before a third clipped his shield.

"Dammit!" Cassian cursed as his fighter spun out, his HUD flickering before he regained control. "These things are everywhere!"

Jax's eyes darted across his HUD, which showed Wraith fighters closing in from all sides. "Stay focused, Cass. We've got to hold them off."

Just then, Commander Dalen's voice cut through the comms, grim and resolute. "This is Commander Dalen. The *Resolute* has taken critical damage. We're losing power to all major systems, and the hull won't hold much longer. I'm giving the order to abandon ship. All hands, evacuate immediately."

Jax's heart sank. The *Resolute* wasn't just a ship—it was home, their base of operations while away from Midway Station. He gritted his teeth, determination solidifying in his chest. "Raptors, new mission: escort the shuttles. Protect them at all costs."

Around the ship, emergency alarms blared, and shuttles launched from the hangars, crammed with as many crew members as they could hold. Escape pods jettisoned from every available hatch as systems continued to fail, but the Wraith drones and fighters were everywhere, closing in like predators scenting blood.

A streak of energy cut across Jax's HUD as a Wraith drone fired on a shuttle, its shields barely holding under the assault. "Marko, Cassian, cover those shuttles! Don't let anything get through!"

The squadron quickly broke into smaller groups, forming protective screens around the escaping shuttles and pods. Rafe led a wing to intercept a squadron of Wraith fighters zeroing in on escape pods, expertly cutting through the enemy with rapid laser fire. One by one, the Wraith fighters exploded, but for every one destroyed, two more seemed to take its place.

"Too many of them!" Rafe shouted. "We're not going to hold them all off!"

Jax swerved to avoid a volley of missiles, his lasers locking onto a drone closing in on the main group of shuttles. His shots hit their mark, shredding the drone into a fireball of debris.

But then, his radar flashed red—a massive Wraith capital ship had entered the fray. Its colossal guns swiveled toward the *Resolute* and opened fire, unleashing a devastating torrent of energy blasts that ripped through the *Resolute's* weakened hull. Explosions erupted across the ship, entire sections tearing off and spinning into space.

"Dalen!" Jax yelled into the comms. "You need to get out of there now!"

"We're going, Jax," Dalen responded, his voice as grim as steel. "But some of my crew are still in escape pods. You have to cover the rescue shuttles—let them collect as many pods as they can."

Jax took a breath, fighting the desperation that clawed at him. "Understood. Raptors, new priority: protect the rescue shuttles and escape pods. We don't leave anyone behind."

As the shuttles continued to ferry crew away from the doomed cruiser, Raptor Squadron risked the debris field, flying close to the wreckage to intercept drones and fighters threatening the evac routes. Their sleek fighters danced through the chaos, their lasers finding targets with deadly precision.

Marko Gale fought with sharp reflexes, weaving between drones and dodging debris from the *Resolute*. His quick maneuvers and pinpoint shots kept him alive in the mayhem as he tore through Wraith drones. But then, a Wraith drone flanked him, firing a missile directly at his ship. The explosion was instant—a blinding fireball erupting around him, his fighter shattered into fragments.

"Marko!" Cassian's voice cut through the comms, raw with shock and horror. But Marko's signal had vanished.

Jax's heart clenched, grief threatening to break his focus. "Stay focused, Cassian," he barked, his voice tight. "We'll mourn later. Keep fighting!"

Cassian's breathing steadied, his voice steadier as he nodded. "Copy that, Jax."

The battle dragged on, Raptor Squadron picking off as many enemies as they could. Their losses were mounting, and the overwhelming waves of drones were slowly but surely breaking through. But the remaining Raptors fought with a desperate resolve, clearing the path for shuttle after shuttle.

Finally, the last rescue shuttle picked up the remaining escape pods, the crew packed tightly inside.

"Shuttles are clear!" Rafe called out. "We've got to jump now, or we're dead!"

Jax took a final, lingering look at the *Resolute,* now little more than a drifting, burning hulk against the starry backdrop. He knew how much had been sacrificed, but there was no time to mourn. "All units, prepare for jump. Get out of here!"

As the remaining fighters and shuttles made a blind jump, space bent around them, carrying them away from the doomed battlefield and into the unknown.

When the squadron exited hyperspace, they found themselves in a desolate system, far from the Wraiths and the wreckage of the *Resolute*. A heavy silence fell over the group. They had escaped, but at a terrible cost.

Jax's comms buzzed as he connected to Commander Dalen, who was on one of the shuttles, packed with survivors. "Dalen, are you alright?"

Dalen's voice was tired but firm. "Most of the *Resolute's* crew made it onto the shuttles. We lost good people today, Jax... but we saved more than I'd hoped, thanks to you and Raptor Squadron."

Jax swallowed hard, the weight of Marko's death still pressing heavily on his chest. "What's next, Commander? The shuttles won't last long out here."

Dalen sighed. "We've only got enough fuel for one more jump. We have to make it count."

Rafe's voice cut in. "I found a system nearby. It used to be inhabited, but it's been quiet since the Empire's war with the Vanguard last year. It could be a risk."

Jax's gut twisted at the mention of the Vanguard. "That area's dangerous territory, Commander. The Vanguard had forces there. If they're still active…"

Dalen paused, weighing their limited options. "We don't have a choice, Jax. If we stay here, we die. If we jump there… maybe we find shelter, supplies, a way out."

Jax took a steadying breath, trying to ignore the dread creeping in. "Understood. We jump."

With a final command, Dalen ordered, "Set coordinates for the system, and let's hope we're not jumping into a Vanguard stronghold. All units, prepare for jump."

The battered remnants of Raptor Squadron and the last of the *Resolute's* shuttles lined up their coordinates, engines flaring to life for one desperate leap into the unknown. With a flash of light, they vanished into hyperspace, leaving behind only memories of their fallen comrades and the lingering hope that some refuge lay ahead.

Chapter 12: Low Fuel

The jump into the unknown system felt like an eternity. When Raptor Squadron and the last shuttles emerged from hyperspace, Jax couldn't shake a creeping sense of foreboding. Below them loomed a desolate world, a once-thriving colony now shrouded in shadow, its cities barely discernible beneath thick clouds that swirled ominously over the surface.

"Welcome to the middle of nowhere," Rafe muttered over the comms, tension thick in his voice.

Jax scanned his console readouts, finding no signs of life or energy sources, no active ships in orbit—just an eerie, pervasive silence. It was unsettling, but their options were limited. The shuttles were nearly out of fuel, and the squadron's fighters were barely holding together after their last brutal encounter.

"Commander," Jax called over the comms to Dalen, "no activity here, but we'd better proceed with caution."

"Agreed," Dalen replied. "We'll land near one of the old colony zones. If we're lucky, we'll find supplies and enough fuel to make the jump home."

With the plan set, the group began their descent. Raptor Squadron flew low over the barren landscape, scanning for any signs of danger. Abandoned buildings and shattered skyscrapers loomed from the planet's surface, remnants of a colony reduced to rubble during the Vanguard conflict. The entire area felt... wrong, as if the planet itself was steeped in dark memories.

As they neared the landing site, Jax noticed Cassian's fighter drifting slightly. "Stay in formation, Cass. We need to land together."

"Sorry, Jax," Cassian muttered, sounding distracted. "This place just... doesn't feel right."

Jax couldn't disagree. "I know, but we don't have a choice. We get in, get what we need, and get out."

The shuttles descended cautiously, landing in the heart of the abandoned city. Their engines sputtered as the last drops of fuel burned through the lines, cutting out with a final, exhausted sigh. Raptor Squadron touched down nearby, keeping weapons systems online in case trouble found them first. A heavy silence settled around them, thick and unnatural.

"All units, secure the area and search for supplies," Dalen ordered. "Stay alert. We have no idea what's still out here."

The crew disembarked cautiously, moving through cracked streets and hollowed-out buildings. Jax led his squadron through the ruins, each of them scanning every shadow and broken window. He couldn't shake the feeling that they weren't alone. He'd left Rafe in his fighter flying a patrol over the area.

Rafe's voice crackled through the comms. "Jax, I'm picking up faint energy signatures. Looks like an old fuel depot up ahead. We might just get lucky."

Jax's spirits lifted. "Send me the coordinates. Let's check it out."

They advanced, but the unsettling sensation only grew as they neared the depot. The surrounding structures were too intact, their facades too clean, untouched by the devastation that had scarred the rest of the city.

"Something's not right here," Rafe's voice came over the comms again, thick with unease. "I've got a bad feeling about this."

Before Jax could reply, the ground trembled violently. Explosions erupted from hidden charges buried beneath the rubble, debris bursting upward in massive plumes. Rafe's fighter rocked under the impact, his shields flaring as he fought to steady the craft.

"Ambush!" Cassian shouted, running back towards his fighter.

The comms erupted with shouted commands as Raptor Squadron scrambled to get their fighters in the air. From the ruins, hidden turrets and automated drones activated, filling the air with deadly laser fire. The entire landing zone had transformed into a trap.

"Get airborne! Now!" Jax yelled, slamming his fighter's controls forward and lifting off in a tight spiral to avoid incoming fire.

The shuttles were under heavy assault, their weakened shields barely holding. Raptor Squadron launched counterattacks, strafing the hidden turrets and drones in an attempt to create a defensive perimeter around the shuttles.

"Commander Dalen, it's a trap!" Jax barked. "We need to evacuate now!"

"We're taking heavy fire," Dalen replied, his voice strained. "Shuttles are lifting off, but we have minimal shielding and no fuel. We won't last long at this rate."

Jax gritted his teeth, dodging a barrage of turret fire while keeping one eye on the shuttles. The drones swarmed them, their shots precise and unyielding. One shuttle took a direct hit, its engines sputtering and sending it veering dangerously close to the ground.

"Jax, we've lost Shuttle Two!" Rafe's voice was filled with horror and frustration.

Jax cursed under his breath. Every loss was a blow they couldn't afford. "Everyone, fall back! Focus on protecting the survivors!"

As they regrouped, a grim realization hit Jax. This wasn't just a random ambush—this trap was premeditated, someone knew they'd be here, knew their situation.

"Jax," Cassian's voice came over the comms, tight with dread, "what if this was the whole plan? We've been led here... to die."

Jax's jaw clenched, his mind racing. "Not today. We're getting out of this."

The odds, however, were against them. The automated defenses continued their assault, and the shuttles were nearing their breaking points. Just as Jax was running out of options, Rafe's voice broke through, charged with renewed hope.

"I found the fuel reserves! They're still intact—enough to power a jump!"

Dalen's voice was quick and commanding. "Send a team to start the transfer. Raptor Squadron, hold the line! We need every second you can give us."

With a renewed sense of purpose, Raptor Squadron formed a tight defensive formation, laying down covering fire against the relentless drones and turrets. The turrets were powerful, but predictable; Jax led precision strikes, taking advantage of each opening as the squadron fired in unison to disable as many drones as possible.

Cassian's voice came through, focused and calm despite the chaos. "Jax, I've got your six."

"Good," Jax replied. "We can't let anything through to the shuttles."

Minutes felt like hours as they fought to keep the drones and turrets at bay. They flew tight, quick patterns through the defenses, firing continuously as they evaded incoming shots. As the last shuttle tank filled with fuel, Rafe's voice came in sharp over the comms.

"Fuel's loaded! We're ready for jump."

Jax didn't hesitate. "Raptors, fall back to the shuttles! Let's get out of here!"

The squadron peeled away from the ruins, fighters damaged but holding together. The shuttles lifted off shakily, their engines straining but functional as they climbed above the city. Jax and the others moved into a tight escort formation, shooting down any drones that tried to follow.

The automated defenses continued to fire, but Raptor Squadron held firm, guiding the shuttles out of range. Finally, the skies cleared, and the turrets fell silent, unable to track them.

"Coordinates locked," Dalen's voice came through, urgent but steady. "Jumping in three... two... one."

Space warped around them, stars stretching and then snapping back as they escaped the trap. When they emerged, they found themselves in the quiet expanse of an empty, forgotten system.

Jax let out a shaky breath, hands trembling on the controls. They had made it. Just barely.

As the shuttles coasted in the void, Jax opened a private channel to Dalen. "Commander, we were set up. Whoever did this knew we'd be there."

Dalen's voice was somber. "I suspected as much. This wasn't random. Someone wants Raptor Squadron out of the picture."

Jax's tone was firm. "Whoever they are, they're not done with us yet. We need to return to Midway Station and regroup. Figure out who's behind this."

"We will," Dalen assured him. "But for now, we survive."

With the precious fuel they'd acquired, the shuttles prepared for the final jump. Their losses were heavy, the crew exhausted, but they'd survived.

"Coordinates set for Midway," Rafe confirmed, his voice filled with relief.

"Jump when ready," Dalen commanded.

With a final flicker of starlight, the battered shuttles and the last of Raptor Squadron vanished into hyperspace, heading back to Midway Station—and toward answers that lay waiting in the heart of the Empire.

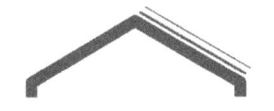

Chapter 13: Fresh Meat

The days on Midway Station had been unnervingly quiet since their last encounter with the Wraiths. Despite the calm, the losses weighed heavily on Jax. Sitting across from Commander Dalen in the dimly lit officer's lounge, he nursed his drink, reflecting on all that had transpired.

"I still can't believe we lost the *Resolute*," Jax said, his voice heavy with regret. The *Resolute* had been more than just a ship; it was Raptor Squadron's home and support vessel, obliterated in the last skirmish. Along with it, they'd lost some of the best pilots Jax had ever flown with.

Dalen leaned back, exhaling slowly, his eyes distant. "Yeah, it's a tough blow, but we have to keep going. Raptor Squadron needs to get back to full strength, and reinforcements are on the way."

Jax looked up, curiosity piqued. "Replacements?"

Dalen nodded, his expression hardening. "A new warship, the *SSV Garrett*, has been assigned to Midway. It's a fast-response vessel with heavy firepower. Captain Thomas Mendez will be in command."

Jax raised an eyebrow, nodding with a hint of approval. "*Garrett*. Sounds solid. And what about Raptor?"

"We're getting two new pilots," Dalen continued. "Sarah Bringi and John McHenry. Experienced, both of them. They'll be reporting to you soon. Also, I've been officially assigned as Midway Station's base commander."

Jax set his drink down, a smile breaking through the somber mood. "Congratulations, Commander. Midway's lucky to have you; you'll make a damn good leader."

Dalen's expression softened. "Thanks, Jax. But there's a lot riding on this. The Wraiths are stepping up their game. It's going to take all we've got to keep this station and Raptor Squadron safe."

They sat in silence, each lost in thought about the battles yet to come, the risks they would face, and the sacrifices that might be necessary.

Two days later, Jax stood in the hangar, watching as the new recruits approached him. Sarah Bringi and John McHenry were both young but carried themselves with the steady confidence of seasoned pilots. They had the look of people who had seen battle and survived it. Jax took in their posture, reading their nerves beneath the stoic exteriors.

"Welcome to Raptor Squadron," Jax said, his tone appraising. "Before we get started, I need to hear about your records and what you think you bring to this team. Start talking."

Sarah Bringi stepped forward first, her stance firm, voice steady. "Sir, I've served in two combat theaters, mostly patrolling the outer sectors. My last assignment was on the *SSV Thompkins,* escorting supply convoys under heavy pirate threat. I have over 200 flight hours, 15 confirmed kills, and extensive experience in defensive maneuvers. I'm a good fit for Raptor Squadron because I know what it takes to survive on the frontier, and I know how to fly smart, not just fast."

Jax nodded, impressed by her poise and self-assurance. "Smart and fast will serve you well out here."

John McHenry stepped forward next, his voice firm and unflinching. "I've served two tours on the *SSV Dominion,* both in planetary defense and capital ship engagements. I've piloted nearly every fighter class in the fleet, and I've had my fair share of close combat encounters, both in the air and on the ground. Raptor Squadron needs versatility and precision, and I'm bringing both."

Jax eyed them critically, his expression unreadable. "You've got the records, but this squadron isn't just about flying. Raptor Squadron is about survival, adaptability, and watching each other's backs when it counts. Prove to me you're more than your stats. Get ready—live drills start soon."

The new recruits nodded, determination sparking in their eyes. They moved off to prepare as Jax turned toward the briefing room, where Commander Dalen was waiting to discuss the squadron's next steps.

Shortly after, Jax entered the briefing room to find Dalen speaking with Captain Thomas Mendez, a tall, muscular man with a firm handshake and a commanding presence. Mendez exuded the quiet confidence of a battle-hardened officer, the kind of man who didn't waste words.

After initial greetings, Mendez launched into the plan. "The *Garrett* will be positioned to support your squadron and Midway with quick-response capabilities. We're equipped with dual ion cannons, heavy torpedoes, and a full contingent of Imperial Marines for ground engagements. If the Wraiths make another move, we'll be ready to hit back hard."

Jax folded his arms, a hint of skepticism in his eyes. "Imperial Marines? That'll be interesting. Historically, pilots and Marines don't exactly see eye to eye."

Mendez smirked, the trace of a smile tugging at the corner of his mouth. "I've heard about that rivalry. But when the bullets start flying, I expect everyone to play nice."

Jax met Mendez's gaze with a steely look of his own. "Raptor Squadron's already lost a lot, Captain. We're not here to make friends with the Marines; we're here to get the job done."

Mendez gave a nod of approval. "Good. I prefer straight shooters. The *Garrett* will focus on securing Midway's defenses. If we need to get in and out of hostile zones, we're fast enough to respond in minutes, and tough enough to bring the fight to them."

Jax took this in, appreciating the *Garrett's* potential to reinforce their operations. "What's the plan going forward?"

Mendez's expression turned cold and determined. "We're ramping up patrols across the sector. The Wraiths need to understand that if they try anything, we'll be ready to hit back hard. With Raptor Squadron running interference, they'll regret even thinking about Midway."

Dalen added, "We're upping our intelligence-gathering operations as well. The Wraiths are unpredictable, but they've shown an unusual interest in this station. We need to be proactive."

Jax nodded, absorbing the scope of the new mission. Raptor Squadron and Midway Station weren't just playing defense anymore—they were a strategic line in the sand.

Elsewhere on the station, Rafe had called Cassian to his quarters, which were cluttered with scattered equipment, tools, and screens showing live camera feeds from across Midway. Rafe sat hunched over a terminal, typing rapidly, his eyes scanning through lines of code with intense focus.

"I've tapped into the station's video and comms systems," Rafe said, gesturing to the feeds. "Got a program running that'll flag any unusual activity. Problem is, when I tried to backtrack the footage from previous incidents… someone wiped the records."

Cassian's face darkened as he processed this. "Wiped? Someone's covering their tracks. But who?"

Rafe looked up, his expression grim. "Whoever it is, they know what they're doing. But with this setup, we'll catch them if they try anything else."

Cassian placed a hand on Rafe's shoulder, a sense of urgency in his voice. "Keep this quiet. If they realize we're onto them, they might escalate."

Rafe nodded, his gaze steely. "Understood. I'll keep you posted."

In the cramped cockpit of a shadowy shuttle hidden in deep space, a figure activated a secure comm link. The console cast a dim glow over his face, hardening his expression as he relayed the situation.

"It's no longer safe to contact you from the station," he said quietly, voice edged with frustration. "Rafe has set up surveillance protocols. He's becoming a problem."

The voice on the other end was cold and commanding. "Then eliminate him. But remember, Cassian is the primary target. Handle this carefully."

The shadowy figure hesitated, then nodded. "Understood. I'll take care of both."

"Remember, we are on a timeline," the voice warned, sharp and impatient. "I expect results."

With a grim look, the shadowy figure closed the comm, leaning back as he calculated his next steps. Soon, the quiet halls of Midway Station would descend into chaos, and he was ready to strike.

Chapter 14: Close Call For The Tech Guy

The simulated VR combat arena was alive with holographic enemies, the hum of starfighter engines, and bursts of laser fire. Raptor Squadron dodged and weaved through the virtual chaos, their sharp movements a testament to their months of combat experience. At the rear were the new recruits, Bringi and McHenry, gripping their controls with tense anticipation as they struggled to keep pace.

"Try to keep up, rookies," came a smug voice over the comm from Cassian, who relished no longer being the newest member. "This isn't babysitting. We don't need dead weight."

Bringi gritted her teeth as she narrowly dodged a plasma bolt, her heart pounding. Ahead of her, McHenry was flying in a tight formation, clearly focused, though he struggled to match the precision of the veterans. The others continued their banter, good-natured but cutting, a test as much as the simulation itself.

"Hey, Bringi, friendly fire's still not allowed," a voice chimed in, teasing as one of her shots went wide, nearly clipping a teammate.

Jax's voice cut through the chatter. "Let 'em breathe, people. We all started somewhere," he said, calm but commanding.

Despite his intervention, the veterans kept up the teasing, their movements through the battlefield smooth and practiced while Bringi and McHenry fought both the simulation and the pressure to prove themselves. By the end, sweat dripped down McHenry's brow as he unclasped his helmet. Bringi let out a frustrated sigh, visibly flustered by the relentless taunts. Cassian and the others walked by, offering smirks, but Jax stopped to place a reassuring hand on McHenry's shoulder.

"You'll get there," Jax said firmly. "Out here, it's about endurance as much as skill. We've all been through it."

McHenry nodded, breathing a sigh of relief. Bringi glanced at him, sharing a look of determination. They'd make it, one way or another.

A few hours later, in the sterile confines of Midway Station's briefing room, Commander Dalen sat at the head of the table, officers gathered around him. Jax took a seat beside Captain Thomas Mendez of the *SSV Garrett*. Across from him sat Imperial Marine Lieutenant Dante, a tall, broad-shouldered man with a reputation for zero tolerance and a piercing stare. His rigid posture conveyed authority, a presence that filled the room with quiet intensity.

Commander Dalen's voice broke the silence, laying out the mission. "The *Garrett* will be conducting patrols in the outer sectors where we've seen recent pirate and Wraith activity. It'll keep the perimeter more secure, reduce incursions, and bolster defense."

Captain Mendez gave a brisk nod. "We've already mapped out potential hotspots. My team is prepped and ready to go. The *Garrett* will be in top condition for any confrontation."

Dalen's gaze shifted to Jax. "Meanwhile, Raptor Squadron will continue VR combat drills and patrols closer to Midway. I need your people sharp and prepared to mobilize on short notice."

Jax nodded but couldn't help noticing Lieutenant Dante's sharp gaze on him. The Marine's silence was heavy, an unspoken tension simmering between them.

"And one more thing," Dalen added, sensing the tension. "I expect full cooperation between the pilots and marines while stationed here. The reports I've read show too much friction. We're all on the same side here."

Jax leaned forward, expression unwavering. "With all due respect, Commander, pilots and marines don't exactly see eye to eye. We've got different approaches to combat. That kind of friction doesn't disappear overnight."

Dante's jaw tightened, his voice cold. "Maybe if pilots didn't treat marines like cleanup crews, we wouldn't have this problem."

Before the argument could escalate, Dalen raised a hand. "Enough. Both of you are leaders here. If your teams see you clashing, what do you think they'll do? Set the example. This isn't optional."

Jax glanced at Dante, whose eyes held a steely defiance, but he nodded. "Understood, Commander."

Dante gave a stiff nod as well. "We'll make it work."

The silence that followed was tense, a silent agreement that despite their differences, they'd cooperate. For now.

Later that evening, in the twisting, dimly lit corridors deep within Midway Station, Rafe knelt under a malfunctioning security camera. The small device had been offline for several hours, a lapse he couldn't afford in his surveillance grid. His fingers moved swiftly, reconnecting wires as he focused on the task at hand. But his mind lingered on a growing list of suspicions; someone was targeting Raptor Squadron.

He didn't hear the footsteps.

A hand clamped over his mouth, and a blade flashed in the muted light, aimed straight for his side. Rafe twisted instinctively, just managing to deflect the worst of the strike, though pain shot through his arm as the knife grazed him. He threw an elbow back, slamming into his attacker's ribs, earning a grunt of surprise.

But the assailant was relentless. He twisted around, tightening his grip and jabbing the blade again. Rafe barely managed to block it, catching the wrist of his assailant. The two grappled, their shadows twisting in the narrow corridor. The blade flashed close to Rafe's throat, inches away as he fought to keep his balance, the silence of the deserted alley amplifying the danger.

Suddenly, a voice shouted from the corridor behind them. "Hey! Get off him!"

McHenry, fresh from the training sim, had heard the struggle as he passed by. Without hesitation, he rushed into the fray, tackling the attacker with full force. The three of them went down in a heap, and McHenry narrowly avoided the blade as it arced toward him. The fight turned chaotic, fists and elbows striking in quick succession.

Rafe managed to secure the assailant's left arm, twisting it back. "Hold him!" he gasped to McHenry, his face twisted in pain.

McHenry pressed his knee into the assailant's shoulder, struggling to control the other arm. The attacker thrashed, wild with desperation, and as they struggled, the blade slipped from his grasp. In the scramble, the knife was driven into the assailant's own side. He let out a choked gasp, his movements weakening as blood began to pool beneath him.

Breathing hard, Rafe staggered back, clutching his injured arm. "Damn... didn't see that coming."

McHenry remained kneeling, eyes wide with shock as he processed the moment. "What... what do we do now?"

Rafe straightened, reaching for his comm. "We call station security. This guy wasn't here by accident."

Minutes later, the corridor filled with the flashing lights of station security and paramedics. The assailant, bleeding heavily but stabilized, was secured, his identity a mystery that only deepened the questions surrounding Raptor Squadron's recent troubles.

Chapter 15: I can Take Care Of Myself

Jax, Rafe, and McHenry stood around the medical bed as the station's medic finished stitching up Rafe's arm. The knife wound had been deep, and Rafe winced as the needle tugged through his skin for the final stitch.

"That should do it," the medic said, stepping back to admire his work. "You'll need to avoid any strenuous activity for the next few days, but given the circumstances, I'm sure you'll ignore that advice."

Rafe flexed his arm slightly, testing the stitches and giving the medic a lopsided grin. "Thanks, Doc. I'll take it easy... as much as I can."

Jax, leaning against the wall with his arms crossed, filled Rafe in on the assailant's status. "Your attacker's still unconscious. Station security says he's in critical condition. They identified him as Creel Stanton—a small-time crook and sometime smuggler. The Imperial Marshal's Office sent over his file."

"Creel Stanton?" Rafe frowned, shaking his head as the name drew a blank. "Why would a low-level criminal risk targeting us? None of this adds up."

Jax shrugged, though a shadow of doubt crossed his face. "Maybe he was hired by someone, or maybe it's completely unrelated."

Rafe scoffed, his voice laced with sarcasm. "The guy tries to knife me in a dark alley, and you think that's a coincidence?"

"I'm just saying we don't know enough to jump to conclusions," Jax replied, his voice calm but firm.

Nearby, McHenry crossed his arms, his expression indignant. "What I want to know is why no one thought to inform Bringi and me that someone's been gunning for Raptor Squadron. Seems like critical intel to leave out."

Jax sighed, rubbing his temples. "We didn't want to cause unnecessary alarm without solid proof. This attack was the first concrete sign that we're being specifically targeted."

"Yeah, well, I'd rather be a little alarmed than blindsided by some knife-wielding lunatic," McHenry muttered.

As they continued discussing the implications of the attack, none of them noticed the shadowy figure slipping through a side door into the infirmary. Dressed in a nondescript maintenance jumpsuit, he moved with the practiced ease of a seasoned infiltrator. His face was obscured by a hood and a shadow-casting visor, concealing his features. Head lowered, he walked with a calm but purposeful stride, heading directly for Creel Stanton's bed.

The infirmary was dim, the quiet broken only by the occasional beep of monitoring machines. The shadowy figure moved with silent precision, checking over his shoulder to ensure he hadn't been spotted. Jax, Rafe, and McHenry remained immersed in conversation on the other side of the room, unaware of his presence.

Reaching into a concealed pocket, the intruder withdrew a small, cylindrical device filled with a clear, viscous liquid. With deft hands, he attached the device to the IV line feeding into Creel's arm, pressing a button to release its contents. His movements were swift and efficient, and within seconds, the device was back in his pocket.

The heart monitor beside Creel's bed continued its steady beeping, showing no immediate signs of distress. The figure lingered for a moment to ensure the slow-acting poison would remain undetected by the medical equipment. Satisfied, he turned and slipped out as quietly as he'd entered.

Once in a secluded maintenance corridor, the shadowy figure pulled a small, alien-looking comm device from his belt, its jagged design unlike anything used by Imperial forces. He activated it, and a distorted voice crackled through the static.

"Is it done?" The voice was cold, precise.

"Creel has been taken care of," the shadowy figure replied in a low voice. "He won't be talking, and nothing can be traced back to us."

"Good. We're moving up the timetable," the voice commanded. "It's time to eliminate Raptor Squadron—every last one of them."

The figure didn't hesitate. "Consider it done. They won't know what hit them."

The line went dead, and the figure pocketed the comm device, vanishing into the shadows of the station.

Cassian walked into the station bar, scanning the bustling room with a practiced eye. The dimly lit space was buzzing with energy—a typical evening scene for Midway Station after a day of patrols and duty shifts. His initial instinct was to turn around and leave when he spotted a group of marines, loud and brash, taking over a section of the bar. Jax's words echoed in his mind: *"No altercations with the marines, period."* The tension between Raptor Squadron and the station's marine contingent had been brewing ever since Lieutenant Dante arrived, and the last thing Cassian wanted was to make matters worse.

He was about to turn on his heel when he noticed Bringi at the bar, surrounded by the same group of marines. They were laughing, drinks in hand, but Cassian quickly picked up on the mocking tone of their conversation. He could see the leering looks and the crude, suggestive remarks being tossed Bringi's way.

"Come on, sweetheart," one of the marines slurred, leaning too close. "You fly one of those tiny fighters, huh? Bet you can handle some real... turbulence." His words were met with laughter from his friends.

Bringi sat with a steely expression, her shoulders tense as she kept her eyes fixed on her drink. Cassian saw the discomfort in her posture, her refusal to engage as the marines kept up their taunts.

Cassian's jaw clenched. He knew Jax's orders, but seeing Bringi surrounded like that, subjected to harassment, didn't sit right with him. Raptor Squadron looked out for their own, and he wasn't about to stand by and do nothing.

Taking a breath, he made his way over, weaving through tables until he reached her side. "Hey," he said, his voice loud enough to cut through the marines' laughter. "You alright, Bringi?"

She glanced up at him, her eyes flashing irritation but also a silent warning. "I'm fine, Cassian. Just having a drink."

One of the marines, a bulky man with a square jaw and a cocky grin, turned toward Cassian. "What's this, her knight in shining armor?" he sneered. "We're just having a little friendly conversation. Right, boys?"

Laughter erupted from the marines, but Cassian's patience was wearing thin.

"I think she's had enough of your 'friendly conversation,'" Cassian replied coldly. "Why don't you back off?"

The atmosphere shifted instantly. The marine squared up, towering over Cassian as he stood. "You got a problem, flyboy?" His voice dropped, any humor gone. "We're just trying to have a good time, and you're sticking your nose where it doesn't belong."

Cassian wasn't intimidated, though he knew the guy had at least thirty pounds on him. "I said, back off."

The marine's smirk faded. With a sudden move, he swung a fist, connecting hard with Cassian's face and knocking him back against the bar. Cassian barely regained his footing before the marine grabbed his jacket, throwing him to the ground.

Cassian scrambled to his feet, adrenaline kicking in as he swung back, landing a punch across the marine's jaw. It only seemed to make him angrier. The marine retaliated with a hard blow to Cassian's ribs, driving the wind out of him as he staggered back, clutching his side.

By now, the bar had erupted into chaos. Patrons stepped back to avoid the scuffle as shouts and curses filled the room. The other marines were egging their friend on, and it looked like they might all jump in. But Cassian wasn't backing down; he wasn't about to let Bringi fend for herself, even if it meant taking a beating.

Just as things were about to spiral out of control, the doors burst open, and station security stormed in. "Alright, break it up!" a security officer shouted, stepping into the fray.

The marine was mid-swing when two security officers grabbed him, dragging him back from Cassian. Another officer stepped between them, holding Cassian back as he caught his breath, blood trickling from his lip.

"That's enough," the officer said sternly, glancing between the two combatants. "You want to spend the night in the brig?"

Cassian wiped the blood from his lip, his gaze steady as he glared at the marine.

The security officer shook his head. "I'm not hauling either of you in, but both your commanding officers will hear about this." He jabbed a finger at the marines. "Get out. All of you."

Grumbling under their breath, the marines reluctantly left, with the one Cassian had fought still casting a dark look as he walked out. The officer then turned to Cassian. "You too, pilot. Leave before I change my mind."

Cassian nodded, taking a steadying breath. He glanced at Bringi, who'd watched the whole thing with a mixture of amusement and frustration. Together, they stepped out into the corridor, the noise of the bar fading behind them.

"That was stupid," Bringi said as soon as they were alone.

Cassian winced, still holding his side where the marine's punch had landed. "I was just trying to help."

Bringi sighed, crossing her arms. "I didn't need you picking a fight. Those marines were trying to provoke me, and ignoring them was working just fine."

Cassian met her gaze, his expression steady despite the bruises forming. "Maybe you didn't need help, but I couldn't just stand there and do nothing."

Bringi's irritation softened slightly. "I can take care of myself, Cassian."

"I know," he replied, his voice firm. "But Raptor Squadron looks out for its own. No one should have to face that kind of crap alone."

She hesitated, her expression softening. "Well, you didn't have to get yourself pummeled over it."

Cassian managed a small, pained grin. "I've had worse."

Bringi rolled her eyes, but there was a hint of appreciation in her voice. "Next time, at least let me get the first punch in."

Chapter 16: Bombs Away

Rafe sat bathed in the dim glow of his monitors, fingers flying across the controls as he combed through hours of station security footage. The events of the past few days had set his instincts ablaze, and he knew the answers had to be hidden in the details. After hours of backtracking Creel Stanton's movements, he finally spotted it: Creel had arrived on Midway Station aboard a freighter named *Vespera*, on the very day of the attack.

"Gotcha," Rafe muttered, his mind racing through the implications. Whoever had hired Creel didn't want him to linger, and *Vespera* might hold the key to finding out why.

Without wasting another second, he headed to find Jax, his urgency barely kept in check. He found him reviewing a holo-report.

"Jax, I need to get on the *Vespera*. There's something more to Creel's story, and I'm betting that ship has answers," Rafe said, his voice low and intense.

Jax looked up, the weight of recent events clear in his expression. "Creel's dead, Rafe. Didn't survive his injuries. Security's already locked down the *Vespera*—they think Creel was behind the attacks on Raptor Squadron. Dalen's handling it by the book."

Rafe crossed his arms, a deep frown on his face. "There's no way Creel orchestrated this alone. He arrived just hours before he tried to knife me. No way he could've planned all this."

Jax raised an eyebrow. "So, you think he's innocent?"

"Innocent? Not by a long shot. But he's no mastermind. If I can access the *Vespera's* comm and nav logs, we might find out who's pulling the strings."

Jax rubbed his temples, clearly torn. "I get it, Rafe, but Dalen's got security on it, and he won't appreciate us going behind his back. We have to follow protocol."

Rafe's jaw clenched, frustration simmering. "Station security will miss something vital, and by the time they figure it out, we'll all be in deeper trouble. Creel was just a pawn."

Jax stared at him, conflict in his eyes, but then shook his head. "Drop it, Rafe. Let it go."

Rafe didn't respond, only turned and walked away, a determined look crossing his face as he pulled out his comm. Minutes later, Cassian and McHenry stood in his quarters, their expressions wary but curious.

Rafe quickly laid out the plan, his voice a low whisper so the station's surveillance didn't pick it up. "I need you two to create a distraction in the hangar. I'll slip onto the *Vespera* while the guard's focused on you."

McHenry looked hesitant, but he nodded. Cassian, however, grinned. "This could be fun. What kind of distraction are we talking about?"

"Nothing too crazy," Rafe replied, "just enough to keep the guard occupied for a couple of minutes. I need a clean window to get in and pull the logs."

Cassian and McHenry exchanged a look, Cassian's grin widening. "We've got this."

In the hangar, Cassian and McHenry positioned themselves near the *Vespera*, close enough to the security officer's post to be within earshot but far enough away to avoid suspicion. Cassian signaled McHenry, a mischievous glint in his eye.

"So, you ever wonder how fast a guy could disassemble and reassemble a blaster rifle?" Cassian said, loud enough for the guard to hear.

McHenry pulled a small dismantled blaster from his jacket and starting an exaggerated "reassembly." The guard perked up, eyeing them suspiciously as Cassian continued to egg McHenry on, occasionally making loud, unhelpful suggestions. Within moments, they had gathered the guard's full attention.

"Oh, no, that's all wrong," Cassian said, shaking his head dramatically. "You're supposed to attach the coil first!"

McHenry feigned frustration, dropping a component with a loud clatter. "Mind your own business, Cassian! I know what I'm doing!"

The guard approached, eyes narrowing as he observed the "technical difficulties" unfolding before him. "What's going on here?" he barked, his voice laced with annoyance.

Cassian turned, giving the guard a disarming grin. "Just a friendly competition. You want in?"

The guard scowled, distracted just long enough for Rafe to slip past them and into the shadows near the *Vespera*'s ramp.

Moving with the practiced ease of someone who knew how to avoid detection, Rafe slipped aboard the *Vespera*. The ship was dark and silent, the only sound his own breathing as he made his way to the cockpit. The hatch slid open with a soft hiss, and he quickly plugged his portable device into the ship's console, beginning the download of the comm and navigation logs.

As the data transferred, something caught his eye: a series of encrypted files marked with station schematics and personnel profiles. He opened one, and his pulse quickened as he saw the level of detail. The files included Midway Station's vulnerabilities, potential escape routes, and profiles on the command staff and Raptor Squadron. Whoever had hired Creel wasn't just after Raptor Squadron—they were preparing for a larger assault on the station itself.

His fingers flew over the device, uncovering a string of encrypted communications between Creel and someone on Midway. The messages dated back to before Creel had arrived, and shortly after their exchange, a large sum of credits had been wired to Creel's account.

"Someone on the inside hired him," Rafe whispered, feeling a chill as he pieced together the evidence.

With the files in hand, he carefully slipped back out of the *Vespera*, managing to avoid detection as he made his way to find Jax.

Rafe found Jax in a briefing room, going over security protocols. Jax's expression darkened as he saw the look on Rafe's face.

"You disobeyed a direct order," Jax said, his voice low with anger.

"I know," Rafe replied, not flinching. "But this was too important to ignore. Creel wasn't behind the earlier attacks. He was hired after those happened. Look," he said, holding up his comm device. "The person who hired him is still here on the station. These files show encrypted communications and a hefty credit transfer to his account."

Jax's face softened, taking in the information, but his irritation was still evident. "Rafe, you went behind my back. This could've gone south quickly."

"I had to," Rafe said, meeting his gaze. "We're out of time for red tape. Whoever hired Creel has plans for an attack—there are files on Midway's schematics, personnel, and escape routes. We need to act now."

Jax exhaled slowly, visibly unsettled. "Alright. We're taking this to Dalen immediately."

Dalen's expression was thunderous as he flipped through the files on Rafe's device. "You violated a crime scene, disobeyed orders, and compromised a sensitive investigation."

Rafe held his ground, his face set in determination. He knew what he'd done, but the information was too important to regret it.

Dalen's scowl gave way to a grim look as he continued reading, his face hardening as he studied the data. "You're lucky you're right," he muttered, then tapped on the station schematics. "If Creel had access to this level of detail, we're looking at a planned assault."

Dalen straightened, the severity of the situation settling in. "Alert station security. Lock down every sector. We're bringing in the *Garrett's* marines to enforce this." He looked to Jax. "Your squadron will sweep the military hangars for any signs of sabotage. Check everything."

Jax nodded, understanding the urgency. "We're on it."

Entering the hangar, Raptor Squadron moved with a sense of unease. Their sleek Predator-Class starfighters lined the walls, shadows cast across their glossy hulls under the stark lighting. Jax led the way, flanked by Cassian, McHenry, and Rafe, who was still scanning through the files he'd uncovered.

"Full sweep," Jax ordered, his voice steely. "Check everything."

The squadron dispersed, each pilot carefully inspecting the fighters and equipment. Rafe focused his scanner on Cassian's ship, running it over the hull with precision. His scanner beeped unexpectedly, drawing his attention.

"Hold up," Rafe said, freezing as he saw a small, black device tucked into a recessed panel near the fighter's power couplings. He leaned closer, eyes narrowing. "This isn't standard equipment. It's a bomb."

The squadron quickly gathered around, Cassian paling as he processed the discovery. "A bomb? Seriously?"

"It's wired into the power systems," Rafe explained, his voice tense. "If you'd powered this up, it would've gone off."

Jax knelt beside him. "Can you disarm it?"

Rafe examined the wiring, grimacing. "I can't. It's too complicated. Plus, there's a timer... and it's already counting down."

Jax's heart sank as he read the timer's display. "How long?"

"Minutes," Rafe replied, barely keeping the fear from his voice. "And it's linked to a proximity sensor. Moving it will set it off."

Jax immediately tapped his comm, his voice tense. "Dalen, we've got a bomb in the hangar, and it's ticking down fast."

Dalen's voice came back, steady but urgent. "We're sending a bomb tech from the *Garrett,* but he's five minutes out."

"He won't get here in time," Jax replied, the timer's countdown mercilessly ticking away.

As they weighed their options, Cassian suddenly spoke up. "We could tether my fighter to another with a tow cable, drag it out of the hangar, and let it explode in open space."

Rafe's eyes widened. "It's risky, but it's our best shot."

Without hesitation, Jax spoke up. "I'll fly the tow ship."

Cassian began to protest, but Jax silenced him with a sharp look. "No debate. Let's move."

Working with lightning speed, they secured a tow cable between the two fighters. Jax climbed into his cockpit, his face set with grim determination.

Once airborne, Jax's voice crackled over the comm. "As soon as we're clear of the station, I'm cutting the cable."

In the hangar, the squadron held their breath, watching as Jax accelerated, pulling Cassian's fighter into open space. The bomb's timer glowed ominously, seconds slipping away. Just outside the station's perimeter, Jax released the cable, letting Cassian's fighter spin away from the station.

Moments later, the bomb detonated in a fiery explosion, a shockwave rippling through the void. Jax's fighter was jolted by the blast, but it remained intact, though visibly shaken.

A collective sigh of relief filled the hangar as Jax's voice came over the comm, ragged but alive. "Jax here... I'm... I'm okay."

But their relief was short-lived as the station's alarms blared to life, and an explosion echoed through Midway's corridors. Red emergency lights flashed, the station descending into chaos as emergency crews scrambled.

Rafe, Cassian, and McHenry exchanged worried glances.

"We just stopped one bomb…" Cassian said, his voice grim.

Rafe's face tightened as he looked toward the sound of the explosion. "There's more. They're already here."

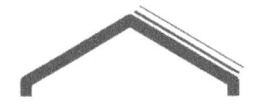

Chapter 17: Midway In Chaos

Amid the blaring alarms and choking smoke filling the corridors of Midway Station, Raptor Squadron felt each explosion reverberate through the deck, the vibrations rattling in their bones. Jax, having been brought back aboard by a repair tug after narrowly escaping the bombed fighter, was already issuing commands with a sense of urgency that cut through the pandemonium.

"Bringi, McHenry," he barked, his voice hoarse but commanding, "take the rest of the squadron and sweep the fighters, top to bottom. Make sure there's nothing else rigged to blow, and get airborne if it comes to that. We could be looking at a full-scale assault."

Bringi nodded, pulling McHenry along toward the docking bay, and the others quickly followed. Their faces, tense and resolute, showed their awareness that a coordinated strike could cripple the station—and their squadron—before they even launched. Meanwhile, Jax turned to Cassian and Rafe, grabbing sidearms from a nearby weapons locker.

"Let's go. We're getting to the bottom of this mess, one way or another," he said, checking the charge on his blaster.

The three of them moved quickly through the corridors, the station continuing to shudder under the onslaught of explosives. Each metallic groan from stressed hull plating echoed ominously, blending with the shouted commands of emergency crews and the hurried footsteps of security personnel and marines dashing through the haze to deal with fires and injuries.

As they neared the hangars, Rafe turned to Jax. "We should check Creel's ship. If someone's covering their tracks, that might be the next target."

Jax hesitated, his eyes hardening, but he nodded, sensing the urgency in Rafe's tone. Cassian gave a silent nod as they pivoted, heading down toward the docking bay where Creel's ship, *Vespera,* was berthed.

When they arrived, they were met with a scene of devastation. The *Vespera* was nothing more than a smoldering husk, a violent explosion having ripped the ship apart. Fire and debris covered much of the bay, and several nearby vessels were badly scarred. Emergency crews worked frantically to contain the blaze, their faces strained with effort as they doused flames and secured loose metal plating.

"By the Emperor…" Cassian murmured, his face pale as he took in the wreckage.

Jax's gaze was unyielding as he scanned the destruction. "This was no accident. Someone wanted to make a point—and erase any evidence Creel left behind."

Rafe looked around warily, leaning in close to the others. "We need to check the surveillance logs in my quarters. If anyone planted those bombs, there's a good chance we'll catch them on camera before they could erase the footage."

Jax and Cassian exchanged a look, and with a nod, the trio slipped away from the chaotic hangar, retracing their steps through the smoke-filled corridors back to Rafe's quarters. The tension in the station was palpable, with smoke and emergency lights creating an eerie atmosphere as crew members darted through the halls, shouting to one another over the roar of the alarms.

Once inside Rafe's quarters, he immediately moved to his terminal, activating his surveillance equipment—a top-notch setup he had meticulously pieced together over his years on the station.

"Alright," Rafe muttered, pulling up footage from the hangar and scanning it frame by frame. "This is just before the explosion."

The grainy footage showed an empty hangar. Then, suddenly, a shadowy figure appeared onscreen, moving with careful precision. He crept toward the *Vespera*, methodically attaching small devices along the hull's edges.

Jax leaned in closer, frowning as he observed the figure's movements. "Who the hell is that?"

Cassian's eyes narrowed as he examined the figure's posture and attire. "I've seen him in the bar a couple of times. Kept to himself, didn't seem like much, but clearly, I was wrong."

The shadowy figure continued his work, his movements coldly efficient as he placed the last explosive and disappeared into the shadows moments before the blast. Rafe froze the footage, studying the man's face, though obscured, his profile faintly visible under the dim light.

"We need to identify him," Jax said, his tone icy. "If he's planting bombs across the station, this is only the beginning."

Rafe's gaze darkened, glancing toward the door. "We need to be discreet. This operation is too organized for us to trust just anyone. He has connections, possibly Wraith allies."

Cassian's jaw clenched. "If he's working with the Wraiths, this could go well beyond just taking out *Vespera*. We might be looking at an attempt to sabotage the whole station."

Jax gripped his sidearm tightly. "No more waiting. Let's find him before he makes his next move."

With renewed urgency, Jax, Cassian, and Rafe slipped out of Rafe's quarters, navigating the twisting corridors of Midway Station. The emergency lights flickered erratically, casting long shadows that seemed to distort with each step they took. The trio moved in tight formation, their senses on high alert, watching every corner as they tracked the shadowy figure's likely path deeper into the maintenance decks.

Jax took the lead, his tall, broad-shouldered frame moving with purpose through the smoky haze. His steely gray eyes were sharp and focused, his years of command shining through in his measured movements. Cassian, younger and quicker, followed close behind, his bright eyes darting around with a mix of eagerness and apprehension, his blaster at the ready. Rafe, bringing up the rear, moved with a cautious step, his mind already calculating their next moves. His blue eyes were cold and focused, reflecting his years of intelligence training as he analyzed every sound and shadow around them.

As they reached an intersection of corridors, Rafe's eyes flicked upward, catching a faint shimmer near the ceiling—a barely perceptible glint of metal. He tensed, his instincts screaming.

"Hold up," he hissed, halting the others.

Cassian followed his gaze, his face paling as he recognized the subtle shapes hidden among the ceiling panels. "Automated turrets… rigged to motion sensors."

Almost on cue, the turrets whirred to life, extending from the panels with lethal precision. The first shot nearly clipped Rafe, who ducked behind a metal crate, narrowly avoiding the scorching red beams. Jax dove into cover, returning fire with steady aim as he tried to disable the closest turret.

"Damn it!" Jax growled, his voice strained. "How did he set this up so fast?"

"This has been in the works for a while," Rafe replied, his tone edged with urgency. "We need to disrupt the motion sensors—now!"

Jax's eyes darted across the corridor, landing on a small maintenance panel just above them. "Cassian! Shoot that power conduit above the turrets!"

Cassian nodded, taking a steadying breath. With careful aim, he squeezed the trigger, and his shot hit its mark. Sparks exploded from the panel, and with a sputtering whine, the turrets powered down, leaving the corridor in silence.

Jax exhaled, glancing at Rafe. "Close call."

Rafe stood up, brushing the dust from his jacket. "He's leading us somewhere. This wasn't random."

"I know," Jax replied, his expression hardening. "But he's running out of places to hide."

They moved forward cautiously, wary of more traps. The station's emergency klaxons blared in the distance, blending with the tension that hung thick in the air. After navigating several winding corridors, they arrived at an isolated storage area on the edge of the maintenance decks, a dimly lit sector rarely visited by anyone outside of station personnel.

The air felt heavier here, thick with the hum of the station's systems and the faint, acrid scent of machinery.

"Stay sharp," Jax whispered, gesturing for Cassian and Rafe to fan out. They moved forward, weapons at the ready.

At the far end of the corridor, they spotted him—the shadowy figure from the footage. He was hunched over a console, his back to them, his fingers moving rapidly as he accessed the system. His dark, nondescript clothing blended seamlessly with the station's dim lighting, and his face was obscured by a hood.

Jax aimed his blaster, his voice a low warning. "Stop right there!"

The figure stiffened, his hands freezing on the console. Slowly, he turned, his face partially visible under the dim light. His eyes, shadowed and intense, met Jax's with a resigned defiance, a bitter smile creeping across his lips.

"Drop it!" Cassian shouted, his voice edged with tension as he stepped closer, weapon raised.

The man's smile widened, almost mocking. "You're too late."

Rafe took a cautious step forward, eyes scanning the man's hands, which hovered dangerously close to his side. "Listen, you don't have to do this. We can figure this out."

But the man's expression didn't change. With a slow, deliberate movement, he raised his hand, revealing a small, cylindrical device clutched tightly in his grip. Jax's eyes widened in alarm, realizing what it was.

"Wait!" Jax shouted, lunging forward.

But the man pressed the device to his chest. A sharp click sounded, followed by a faint hiss. His body went rigid as the toxic chemical surged through his system, his eyes rolling back as he collapsed to the floor, lifeless.

Cassian knelt beside him, checking for a pulse but finding none. "He's dead."

Jax holstered his weapon, frustration etched across his face. "Damn it... we needed him alive."

Rafe knelt beside the body, quickly rifling through the man's pockets. He pulled out a small data pad, its screen flickering with encrypted files. "We might still have a lead here," he muttered, scanning the device.

Jax looked down at the lifeless body, the weight of the day's events pressing heavily on his shoulders. "We need to get this back to command. If he was working with the Wraiths, this is only the beginning."

As they turned to leave, the tension hung heavy between them, knowing they had narrowly stopped a disaster but were still shadowed by the larger threat of the Wraiths. They had thwarted this attack, but somewhere out in the vast reaches of space, the Wraiths were watching, waiting, and planning their next strike.

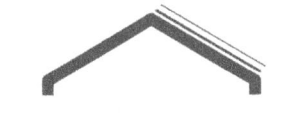

Chapter 18: Intel Briefing

The briefing aboard the *Garrett* was steeped in tension, a sense of secrecy pervading the dimly lit room. Midway Station, once bustling with activity, now floated quietly in space, its systems mostly offline save for a few crews attempting to repair the damage from the recent bombings. Civilians had been evacuated to nearby transports, leaving only a skeleton crew behind to manage the repairs. The primary command staff, including Jax, Commander Dalen, and Captain Mendez, had relocated to the *Garrett*, which was temporarily serving as a command center.

Inside the *Garrett*'s conference room, a large holoprojector flickered to life, illuminating the stern face of Colonel Mitel from Imperial Intelligence. His hologram stood tall, his sharp features enhanced by the cold blue light of the projection.

"Colonel Mitel," Dalen greeted, standing at attention with the rest of the officers. Jax and Mendez stood to his left, dressed in their flight uniforms, their expressions a mix of fatigue and focus, shadows under their eyes from sleepless nights spent securing the station.

"Gentlemen," Mitel began, his voice steely. "Everything you are about to hear is classified. This information does not leave this room. Understood?"

Jax, Dalen, and Mendez nodded in unison. There was no mistaking the gravity of the situation.

"During the Vanguard crisis last year," Mitel continued, his gaze sweeping over the men, "cybernetic soldiers from Old Earth infiltrated Imperial space. These weren't ordinary machines but some of the most advanced, dangerous AIs we've ever encountered. The Vanguard manipulated pirate gangs across the frontier, and the Wraiths were entirely taken over."

Jax's jaw tightened. He remembered rumors of the Vanguard crisis from his time on the frontier, stories of how Rangers Cole Butler and Wes Antrim had fought to neutralize several Vanguard units. But to hear that these AI-controlled soldiers could embed themselves within gangs was a troubling escalation.

"Rangers Butler and Antrim managed to neutralize Vanguard Prime, the leader," Mitel said, his tone tinged with reluctant respect. "But three Vanguard units remain unaccounted for. Their locations are unknown to Imperial Intelligence."

Mendez shifted uncomfortably, exchanging a wary glance with Jax. They'd dealt with pirates and smugglers before, but this was different—something far more calculated.

"Our latest intelligence suggests that one of these missing Vanguards has resurfaced," Mitel stated grimly. "We believe it has reasserted control over the Wraiths, possibly driving their sudden technological advances and militaristic precision. However, we still don't know why Raptor Squadron has been specifically targeted."

Jax clenched his fists, a flicker of anger in his eyes. "We've lost good people, Colonel. What does this Vanguard want with us?"

Mitel's gaze met Jax's. "That's what we're trying to determine, Captain. Raptor Squadron's missions, your close proximity to Midway, or possibly something else—we're not ruling out any variables. But I assure you, Captain, we're investigating every angle."

He paused, letting the weight of his words sink in, then turned to Dalen. "Regarding the figure who took his own life upon discovery—Imperial Intelligence has very little information on him. There's no record in Imperial databases, no criminal background. He's a ghost."

Commander Dalen crossed his arms, his frown deepening. "If he's not in the system, he must have been off the grid for a long time."

Mitel nodded. "The Wraiths have always operated on the fringes, and this man was clearly highly trained, possibly part of a larger organization. His suicide complicates matters, but we will get answers."

Jax exchanged a look with Mendez, whose expression had darkened with the implications. The Wraiths were no longer just a band of pirates; they were part of a much larger, more sophisticated threat.

"For now," Mitel said, voice firm, "the *Garrett* will remain at Midway while repairs are underway. The station should be operational within the month, barring further incidents. Until then, we'll monitor all activity in the sector closely."

Jax stepped forward, his gaze intense. "And if the Vanguard is indeed controlling the Wraiths again, they'll make another move. What's our contingency?"

Mitel's hologram flickered as he seemed to consider his next words carefully. "You're right to be concerned, Captain. This Vanguard is a patient, calculated threat. But we won't be caught unprepared. Intelligence is actively monitoring every signal and transmission from this sector. When they show themselves again, we will respond accordingly."

"How certain are we that it's the Vanguard controlling the Wraiths again?" Dalen asked, his voice carrying an edge of skepticism.

Mitel paused, clearly weighing his response. "Nothing is certain, Commander."

Jax interjected, his voice measured. "If there's any chance it isn't the Vanguard, we need to be sure. We can't afford to be blindsided if we're wrong about the source of this threat."

Mitel's expression tightened. "Rest assured, we are pursuing all possible leads. There are... differences between what we're seeing now and what we observed during the previous engagements with the Vanguard. But the Wraiths are the only faction with the infrastructure for this level of threat. Until we find evidence otherwise, we are proceeding under the assumption that this is Vanguard-related."

Mitel delivered his final order, his tone brooking no argument. "You will receive further instructions when we have more intelligence. For now, focus on repair and regrouping efforts. Do not engage the Wraiths without authorization. This operation is beyond the scope of any one squadron."

As Mitel's hologram flickered and disappeared, a heavy silence filled the room. Jax exhaled slowly, his mind racing with the implications. They weren't dealing with typical pirates; the Wraiths had become pawns in a much larger game. And somehow, Raptor Squadron was at the center of it.

Dalen broke the silence, his voice steely. "We've handled a lot on the frontier, but this... this is something else. We need to be ready."

Jax nodded, determination hardening in his eyes. "We'll be ready, sir."

The three men exited the conference room, each carrying the weight of the briefing. They had narrowly averted disaster with the bombings on Midway, but they all knew the real battle lay ahead. Somewhere in the vastness of space, the Vanguard was out there, waiting for their next move.

In the crew lounge aboard the *Garrett*, Cassian sat alone, fingers drumming absently on the armrest of his chair. The room was dim, only the low hum of the ship's systems filling the silence. He glanced around, noting the emptiness of the room, the blue ambient lighting casting a faint glow that added to the surreal sense of calm. It felt like the lull before another storm, the quiet after the chaos of Midway's bombings.

Bringi sat across from him, her hair pulled back into a simple ponytail, her hazel eyes fixed on him. Cassian had grown to rely on her calm presence amidst the tumult, her wit and steadiness a grounding force in the midst of the chaos. She was sharper than most, quick with a plan, and, Cassian thought, always seemed to know exactly what to say—except now.

Bringi broke the silence first, her voice soft. "It's strange, isn't it? Everything feels quiet now, but it's like we're waiting for the other shoe to drop."

Cassian nodded, shifting uncomfortably. "Yeah, like we're still in the middle of it, even if it feels calm now. I can't shake the feeling there's more coming, and soon."

Bringi leaned back, arms crossed as she studied him. "You're not wrong. The Wraiths, the Vanguard... they're not going to just disappear. And now that we know they're targeting Raptor, we're all still in the thick of it."

Cassian exhaled slowly, feeling the weight of her gaze. He'd always admired her composure under fire, her steady hand, but sitting across from her now, he found himself more nervous than he'd ever been in battle.

"Look, Bringi," he started, his voice faltering. "I... I'm really glad you're here. After everything that's been happening, it's just... it's good to have someone I can trust."

She gave him a warm smile, her eyes softening. "I feel the same way, Cassian. We've all been through a lot, and you've handled it better than most rookies would."

He laughed, a faint, self-deprecating sound. "I don't know about that. I'm just trying to keep it together. Some days, it feels like... like I'm barely keeping my head above water."

"Believe me, I know the feeling," she replied, her voice gentle. "But you're stronger than you think. You've proven that already."

Cassian's heart raced, and he felt a surge of courage. He'd been wanting to tell her something for weeks, ever since they started flying together. She'd become more than just a fellow pilot; she was a friend, maybe something more. But the words felt stuck in his throat, caught between fear and hope.

For her part, Bringi noticed his hesitation, sensing there was more he wanted to say. She'd seen the way he looked at her when he thought she wasn't watching, heard the way his voice softened when they spoke alone. And though she'd been trying to keep things professional, she couldn't deny the way her heart raced when they were together like this. Silently, she wished he'd just say what she suspected he felt.

But Cassian, at the last moment, held back, offering only a faint smile. "Thanks, Bringi. It... it means a lot, hearing that from you."

She nodded, though there was a hint of disappointment in her eyes that she quickly masked with a smile. "Anytime, Cassian."

They sat in companionable silence for a moment longer, the unspoken words hanging between them, each wondering what might happen if one of them just took that final step. The hum of the ship filled the room, wrapping them in a stillness neither seemed ready to break.

Chapter 19: A Mystery Revealed

Weeks had passed since the bombing of Midway Station, and Raptor Squadron had been riding out a temporary calm aboard the *Garrett*. Repairs on the station proceeded on schedule, and no Wraith activity had surfaced anywhere in the Empire. For now, at least, the danger felt distant. Yet a quiet tension lingered, as the squadron knew all too well that this peace was likely just the calm before the storm.

Cassian and Bringi had settled into a morning ritual, sharing breakfast in the *Garrett*'s mess hall. Their conversations grew more relaxed each day, full of laughter and easy banter, and their connection had deepened far more than either had anticipated. But despite their closeness, neither revealed their true feelings. Cassian's nervousness held him back, and Bringi, though she silently wished he'd take the next step, remained patient, watching him with her usual calm.

One morning, as they sat across from each other, the routine felt almost normal, as though the dangers that once surrounded them were a distant memory. But far from the quiet of the *Garrett*, something was stirring in the dark reaches of Wraith-controlled space.

In a remote region within Wraith territory, a female captain sat confidently in her command chair aboard a sleek, advanced warship. Her piercing gaze fixed on an intelligence update flashing on the holo-screen, listing Midway Station's progress, Raptor Squadron's status, and, most notably, details about Cassian.

Her lips pressed into a thin line as she reviewed the report, tapping her fingers rhythmically on the armrest. After a moment, she stood and crossed the bridge, entering her ready room as the doors hissed shut behind her. The soft glow of holo-screens cast sharp shadows across the room's dark walls.

Moments later, one of her officers entered. Tall, with a sleek black uniform and cold, calculating eyes, he bowed his head in deference to his captain.

"Captain," he said, voice low and measured. "The latest intelligence on Raptor Squadron has arrived. Our agent on Midway Station is no longer in play. We'll need to adjust our strategy."

The captain's eyes narrowed as she faced the star map projected before her, her back to the officer. "Yes," she replied. "We anticipated this. It's a setback, but nothing more. Midway remains the key to everything."

The officer took a step closer, a hint of caution in his tone. "With our agent gone, monitoring their movements closely will be difficult. Perhaps it's time to send in a deep-cover operative—allow the AI to implant them within Raptor Squadron."

The captain turned, her face unreadable, eyes gleaming with a dangerous intensity. "That would take too long. We're running out of time."

The officer inclined his head, acknowledging her frustration. "There is another option, Captain. Perhaps it's time to reveal our fleet to the Empire. With the ships we've built, Midway Station would fall swiftly. And we could eliminate Cassian once and for all."

She regarded him for a long moment, his words triggering a deep, personal need beyond her master plan. Cassian. The name lingered in her mind like an unresolved ghost from her past. Cassian had to die. But could she afford the risk of exposing her fleet too soon?

"Perhaps," she said finally, her voice cold and distant. "Perhaps it's time."

The officer bowed, sensing his captain had much to consider. "As you command, Captain. I'll prepare for whichever course of action you decide."

He turned to leave, pausing at the door to look back at her. "Captain Bringi," he said, her name slipping from his lips with quiet familiarity. "Whatever happens, we will see this through. Cassian's end is inevitable."

Captain Bringi turned away, eyes back on the star map, her thoughts heavy. "Dismissed," she said, her voice soft but firm.

As the door closed behind him, she remained alone, the only sound the faint hum of the ship's systems. She was no longer the Bringi Cassian once knew; she was something new, a woman shaped by betrayal, vengeance, and a plan more intricate than anyone in the Empire could fathom.

But one thing was certain. Cassian had to die. And soon.

Chapter 20: In For A Hell Of A Fight

Cassian sat in the cockpit of a Shadow-Class recon fighter, stars streaking past as the small squadron moved through deep space in full stealth mode. The hum of the fighter's systems was faint, masked by advanced stealth tech that rendered them invisible to almost any sensor. His eyes scanned the readouts, his heart steady but alert. This mission felt different—heavier, more dangerous. Then again, most missions felt that way these days, and Cassian always felt uneasy flying anything other than his usual Predator-Class fighter.

He had been assigned to lead Shadow Squadron to scout the systems between Wraith-held space and Midway Station. With the *Garrett* stationed at Midway to protect it during repairs, this mission was vital in detecting potential threats before they escalated. Cassian maintained strict comm silence as he led the squadron deeper into the uncharted fringes of Imperial space.

After hours of scouting, drifting silently through system after system, they saw it.

A fleet.

Cassian's breath caught as the first of the ships came into view. His systems pinged quietly in his headset, identifying a growing cluster of vessels ahead. This was no small convoy or scattered raiding party; this was far larger. The jagged hull designs of the Wraith ships were unmistakable, but what sent a chill through Cassian was what he saw next.

Vanguard capital ships.

Massive and imposing, their sleek, predatory forms moved silently through space, a stark reminder of the Vanguard's power. How could they have amassed such a fleet so quickly after their last crippling defeat?

Then his sensors detected something else: a ship unlike any he'd ever seen. Towering above the rest of the fleet, it had an utterly foreign design. Its dark hull was lined with intricate, almost organic patterns, as if it had been grown rather than built. Cassian refocused his scans, trying to gather data on this unknown ship. Immense and beyond Vanguard size, his sensors struggled to identify its origin or purpose.

Cassian's hand hovered over the controls, his pulse quickening. They needed intel, but detection was not an option. He tapped the comm channel, transmitting on the secure squadron frequency.

"Shadow Squadron, gather all the data you can, especially on the larger ships. We need to stay silent and avoid detection at all costs," he whispered.

His HUD lit up with acknowledgments from his fellow pilots as the squadron fanned out, moving with silent precision to scan the massive fleet from afar. Each second stretched out, the tension mounting as they gathered critical intel.

Finally, Cassian had what they needed. His heart raced as he signaled the squadron to return. Without a word, Shadow Squadron jumped to lightspeed, leaving the terrifying fleet behind.

Back aboard the *Garrett*, Cassian stood before Jax, Dalen, and Mendez in the briefing room, the tension thick as he delivered his report: the fleet's size, the Vanguard capital ships, and the enormous, unknown vessel. The officers listened intently, their expressions grim.

When he finished, Jax exchanged glances with the others. "You're dismissed, Cassian. And remember, you're not to discuss this with anyone. Understood?"

Cassian nodded, a weight settling in his gut. "Understood, sir."

As he left, the weight of what he'd seen clung to him. Something about that fleet felt more dangerous than anything they'd faced before. But he knew better than to press for answers. For now, all he could do was wait.

Once he was gone, Jax turned to Dalen and Mendez, his voice low and urgent. "We need to get this to Imperial Intelligence. Now."

Dalen nodded. "Agreed. Let's get Colonel Mitel on the holo."

Moments later, Colonel Mitel's image flickered into view, his expression stern as he listened to their report. As Jax described the fleet and the data gathered, Mitel's face darkened.

"This can't be," Mitel muttered. "The Vanguard and Wraiths couldn't have rebuilt so quickly. We crippled them last year."

Mendez leaned forward, his voice level. "We have the sensor logs, Colonel. The data doesn't lie. And as far as I understood, the Empire only ever had estimates on the Vanguard's true fleet strength."

Mitel wrestled with the information, finally sighing heavily. "You may be right, Mendez. If they've rebuilt, this is a far bigger threat than we anticipated."

He paused, his expression hardening. "I'll coordinate with the Imperial Navy to reroute reinforcements to Midway Station. But listen closely—under no circumstances are you to operate near that fleet. Hold position and wait for reinforcements. Clear?"

Jax nodded. "Crystal clear, Colonel."

Mitel's image held their gaze. "Good. Reinforcements will arrive soon. Until then, be ready. If that fleet makes a move, we must be prepared for anything."

The holo went dark, and the room fell silent.

Jax turned to Dalen and Mendez, his expression grim. "We're in for a hell of a fight."

Dalen crossed his arms, his brow furrowed. "And I'm not sure we'll be ready for it."

The days passed, and space around Midway Station filled with the Empire's growing might. Cassian watched from a viewport aboard the *Garrett* as capital ships, fighter carriers, and supply vessels streamed in, casting shadows over the still-repairing Midway Station. The sight was awe-inspiring—and a grim reminder of the threat they were facing.

The largest of all, the Imperial dreadnought *SSV Destiny*, loomed like a titan. The *Destiny*, flagship of the fleet, symbolized Imperial strength, its dark hull bristling with weaponry. Cassian had heard stories of the dreadnought's role in past victories. Now its presence added fuel to the rumors spreading through the *Garrett*.

Raptor Squadron buzzed with speculation. The secrecy surrounding their recent scouting mission, combined with the sudden arrival of Imperial forces, stirred rumors. Some speculated that the Wraiths had somehow accessed advanced technology from Imperial vaults. Others whispered of an even greater force lurking, waiting to strike.

But it was the rumors of the Vanguard's resurgence that unsettled Cassian most. The Vanguard capital ships he'd seen weighed heavily on his mind. The Empire had believed them nearly wiped out. But what if they were wrong?

A sharp buzz from his commlink interrupted his thoughts. Jax's voice came through, clipped and serious.

"Cassian, report to the briefing room. Now."

Cassian hurried through the corridors and arrived to find Jax, Dalen, and Mendez already seated. The usual camaraderie was replaced by solemn intensity.

Admiral Hall's image flickered to life on the holo-display, his uniform crisp, his face lined with years of experience. His voice was calm, but the weight of the situation was clear.

"Lieutenant Jax, Commander Dalen, Captain Mendez," Admiral Hall greeted them, nodding to Cassian. "We've assembled a substantial portion of the Imperial fleet around Midway Station. This isn't a show of force—it's a response to an existential threat."

Jax leaned forward. "Sir, is this about the Vanguard?"

Hall nodded. "Yes. The intelligence you provided about the fleet, Vanguard capital ships, Wraith vessels, and an unknown ship has been confirmed. The Empire has monitored Vanguard activity since their last defeat, but we never expected them to rebuild this quickly—or with such strength."

Mendez folded his arms. "But how? We took out Vanguard Prime last year. How could they have resources to build a fleet this size?"

Hall's expression darkened. "It seems we underestimated them. Rogue elements may have funneled resources to the Vanguard. And the unknown ship you encountered, Lieutenant Gray, is beyond anything we've ever seen. If it's leading the fleet, this threat is greater than we anticipated."

Dalen shook his head. "That ship didn't look like anything I've seen. Could it be another faction?"

Hall's voice grew quieter. "We don't have confirmation, but there are theories. Imperial Intelligence believes the unknown ship could be from technology predating even the Vanguard—something ancient."

The room fell silent. An ancient threat, with power enough to rival Imperial tech. Cassian tried to piece it together.

Admiral Hall continued. "This fleet is here to hold the line at Midway. We don't know the Vanguard's plan, but reinforcements are coming. Make no mistake, we are preparing for war."

Jax nodded. "Our orders, sir?"

"For now, defensive positions only. No engagement until we understand their plan. I'll coordinate with Imperial Intelligence and High Command. If the Vanguard moves, we'll be ready."

With that, Hall's image disappeared, leaving the room silent.

Cassian leaned back, mind buzzing. The Empire was preparing for war, and the Vanguard and Wraiths were gathering their strength.

As Cassian left, he couldn't shake the feeling that there was more to this. The unknown ship, the way it led the fleet... something didn't sit right.

Whatever came next, he would be at the heart of it.

Chapter 21: The Battle Of Midway Station

The space around Midway Station crackled with the energy of a brewing storm. For three tense weeks, the Imperial fleet had been bracing for this inevitable clash, every passing day amplifying the suspense. Now, their fears had materialized. Hundreds of enemy ships emerged from hyperspace just outside the defensive perimeter. It was a mismatched but terrifyingly formidable armada: Wraith fighters darted alongside Vanguard destroyers, while gunships and freighters moved in loose but organized attack formations. And, hovering ominously behind them all, was the massive, unknown ship that had haunted Cassian's thoughts since he'd first seen it.

Cassian sat in the cockpit of his Predator-Class fighter, his heart pounding as he watched the enemy fleet advance. The cockpit was dark, illuminated only by the faint glow of his instrument panel. Raptor Squadron had launched as soon as the alarm sounded, and now they hovered just above the *Garrett*, awaiting orders.

"Look at the size of that thing," Rafe muttered over the comms, his voice tight with unease as the enemy ships came into full view. "We're outnumbered two to one."

Before anyone could respond, a chilling broadcast cut through the comms on all known frequencies.

"This is the commander of the Wraith fleet," an icy, distorted voice announced. The transmission revealed a figure cloaked in a dark hood, her face shrouded, sitting calmly on the bridge of the massive unknown ship. "I have no desire for pointless bloodshed. I want Midway Station and Lieutenant Cassian Gray. Relinquish them, and I will guarantee the safety of your fleet. Refuse, and your Empire will burn."

Silence fell over the Imperial fleet, the weight of her words heavy as if the entire armada held its breath. Cassian felt a chill at the mention of his name, his eyes darting to the massive ship in the distance. This was personal.

"Admiral Hall to all Imperial forces," the admiral's stern voice came over the open channel, his tone resolute. "We do not negotiate with terrorists. Your demands are rejected. The Empire stands united."

The unknown captain's laugh echoed across the comms, sinister and amused. "The Vanguard is dead, Admiral. This fleet is my creation, built from the ashes of your failures. My forces will crush your defenses, and Midway Station will be mine."

The transmission cut, and for a tense moment, the battlefield was silent. Then, with a crackle of energy, the enemy fleet surged forward and began firing.

The space around Midway Station erupted into chaos. Fighters from both sides streaked through the void, trails of glowing exhaust marking the path of deadly dogfights. Raptor Squadron led the charge, their nimble starfighters weaving between the heavier Imperial gunships to intercept waves of enemy Wraith fighters.

"Stay sharp!" Jax barked over the comms as Raptor Squadron plunged into the fray. "Pick your targets and watch each other's backs!"

Cassian's pulse quickened as he locked onto an approaching Wraith fighter. His targeting reticle blinked red, and with a pull of the trigger, his laser cannons blazed. The Wraith fighter exploded in a flash of fire, but there was no time to celebrate. More enemies closed in, forcing him and his squadron into relentless engagements.

Rafe's fighter twisted beside him, the two moving in unison, dodging a barrage of laser fire as they looped around an enemy gunship. "These guys just keep coming!" Rafe grunted, narrowly avoiding a direct hit.

Meanwhile, the capital ships clashed in a titanic struggle. The *Garrett* held its position near Midway Station, its turbolasers firing steady volleys as it engaged a pair of Vanguard destroyers. The *Destiny*, the Empire's flagship, unleashed devastating broadsides, tearing into the heart of the Wraith fleet. Imperial frigates and cruisers poured fire into the enemy ranks, but for every ship they destroyed, another seemed to take its place.

For a moment, the Empire held the line. Then, the massive unknown ship, which had so far hung back, joined the fray.

The vessel moved with terrifying grace, its sleek hull gleaming against the fiery backdrop of battle. Cassian felt a chill as it drew closer, casting a long shadow over the battlefield.

"Look at that thing..." Cassian murmured as the unknown vessel dwarfed even the *Destiny*, showing no signs of slowing.

Without warning, the ship unleashed its weapons. A beam of searing energy erupted from its bow, cutting through space and slamming into one of the Imperial destroyers. The destroyer's shields held for a brief second before collapsing, and the ship exploded in a fiery burst, debris scattering in all directions.

"They've got some kind of superweapon!" Jax shouted as the squadron broke from their engagements to reassess the threat. "No Imperial ship can handle that kind of firepower."

The unknown ship continued its merciless assault, each blast reducing an Imperial vessel to floating wreckage. The Empire's most advanced weapons barely registered against the vessel's shields.

"We're getting torn apart!" Rafe yelled as another cruiser exploded nearby.

Cassian's mind raced as he watched the carnage. They were losing, and fast. Nothing they had could penetrate the unknown ship's defenses, and it was systematically dismantling the Imperial fleet.

"Cassian, fall back!" Jax's voice was sharp with urgency. "We can't let them capture you. Retreat to Gaia Prime. That's an order."

Cassian gritted his teeth. "We can't just leave them! I can—"

"That's an order!" Admiral Hall's voice cut in, heavy with finality. "We can't lose you, Cassian. For whatever reason, you're critical to them. Until we understand why, you must escape. Now!"

Cassian hesitated, torn between duty and the urge to fight. His instincts urged him to retreat and regroup. But as he watched his fellow pilots and comrades in danger, something inside him rebelled. He couldn't just run.

As Raptor Squadron prepared to fall back, Cassian switched to a private channel, cutting off communication. An idea—a dangerous, reckless one—formed in his mind. He could still fight. He had to.

With a deep breath, Cassian pushed his fighter into full throttle, breaking formation and angling toward the massive unknown ship. He opened a wide-band transmission.

"This is Lieutenant Cassian Gray of Raptor Squadron. I know you're looking for me. Well, here I am."

A beat of silence.

Then, his fighter jolted as it was ensnared in a powerful tractor beam. Cassian's heart pounded in his chest as the energy field locked onto his ship, pulling him toward the massive vessel.

His plan had worked. But as the enemy ship loomed larger and larger in his viewport, he couldn't shake the wave of dread washing over him.

He was in their grasp now.

Chapter 22: Revelations

Cassian's fighter landed with a soft thud in the enormous hangar of the enemy ship. As he powered down the systems, a creeping sense of dread overcame him. What had seemed like a noble, self-sacrificing plan—surrendering himself to spare the Imperial fleet at Midway—now felt like a grave miscalculation. The hangar stretched out before him, dimly lit with cold, sterile lighting that cast an eerie glow over the rows of soldiers stationed at strict intervals. Their movements were precise, almost mechanical, and Cassian instantly recognized the unnerving rigidity he had seen once before, during the brief but brutal war with the Vanguard. These were not human soldiers; they were likely repurposed Vanguard combat units, coldly efficient and emotionless.

As he unbuckled himself, Cassian's instincts screamed for him to turn, to fight, to find a way back to his fighter and escape. But the surrounding soldiers formed a formidable perimeter as he stepped out, their unblinking visors and mechanical stances conveying no hint of emotion or intent. The squad of robotic guards closed in, their movements silent and fluid, enclosing him in a formation that left him no option but to follow. The air was thick with the faint hum of advanced machinery, laced with a chill that seemed to seep into his bones, making every breath feel colder, more isolated.

They led him from the hangar and down a series of dimly lit corridors. The passageways were lined with smooth, dark metal, unmarred by signs of life—no insignia, no personal touches, only the austere, functional designs of a warship dedicated solely to its purpose. Cassian glanced at the subtle blue lights embedded along the walls, likely indicating energy conduits or data feeds, though they seemed almost organic in their layout, snaking around the metal surfaces like veins in an alien body. Each corridor branched into others in a maze-like fashion, making it impossible to know how deep they were taking him. This was no ordinary vessel; it was a war machine with a foreboding efficiency that left no room for error.

Cassian's mind spun with questions. Who was commanding this fleet? And why had they sought him out specifically? He sensed there was something uniquely sinister about this unknown ship's power, something beyond anything the Empire had encountered. Every footstep echoed, amplifying the stillness that pressed against him like a heavy weight.

After what felt like an eternity, they arrived at a set of massive double doors, which slid open with a low, ominous hiss. Cassian stepped through and found himself on a vast bridge. Dim lighting and cold metal walls surrounded the room, casting shadows that flickered over the sleek, advanced holo-screens lining the perimeter. Tactical readouts projected blue and green hues onto the cold floor, displaying the raging battle outside in minute detail. In the center, surrounded by an air of authority, stood a figure in a dark cloak.

Cassian froze, his breath catching in his throat as the figure turned to face him. His eyes widened in shock. The woman standing before him bore a striking resemblance to Bringi—his Bringi—but older, her features sharper, her expression lined with a bitterness and a coldness that hadn't been there before. Her eyes, once so full of life, were now icy and hardened by what looked like years of experience and grief.

"You... You look like..." Cassian stammered, struggling to process the sight before him.

"Your sweetheart?" she interrupted, her voice laced with barely restrained contempt. "Yes, I look like her, don't I?"

Cassian stood frozen, mind racing as a thousand questions flooded him, but words eluded him. How was this possible?

"You must be wondering why," she continued, stepping closer, her gaze piercing through him. "Why I look like the woman you're so fond of. There's a reason for that."

She motioned for him to follow as she strode toward her ready room. The doors slid open, revealing a stark, personal space devoid of warmth or sentimentality. Dark, streamlined surfaces filled the room, with a few datapads arranged in perfect order on a cold metal desk. The walls were bare save for a holo-map of the galaxy and a single, sharp, vertical line running down one wall, which looked almost like a scar on the ship's otherwise smooth interior. She took a seat behind the desk, folding her hands as her intense gaze fixed on him.

"I've waited a long time for this moment," she said, her tone deliberate and controlled, each word carrying a weight that made Cassian's skin crawl. "A very long time."

Cassian remained silent, his mouth dry, struggling to comprehend what was happening. What he'd intended as a sacrifice for the Empire now felt like a snare—something far larger, more sinister, than he could have imagined.

"This ship, the *Vindicta*, and I are not from this time," she said, leaning back with a faint, almost mocking smile.

Cassian blinked, confusion and disbelief mingling in his mind. "Not... from this time?"

She nodded. "Yes. We come from the near future. A future where you, Cassian, betray Raptor Squadron. You abandon everyone—everyone but me. The younger me, that is."

Cassian's chest tightened. "That's impossible. I would never—"

"Oh, but you will," she interrupted, her voice thick with scorn. "You'll abandon them, and it will cost countless lives. I'm here to prevent that."

His thoughts spun, but the pieces refused to connect. "Why would I..."

"I transferred to Imperial Intelligence after that day," she continued, dismissing his protests. "I couldn't stay with Raptor Squadron after what you did. Then, during a mission, I discovered something—a hidden station, deep within what was once Vanguard space. It lay cloaked in a nebula, untouched for decades."

Cassian's brow furrowed; her words stirred a distant familiarity.

"Of course, I wasn't the first to find it," she added with a cold smile. "Two Imperial Rangers, Butler and Antrim, filed a report on it years ago, but the Empire never followed up. I did. And I found something extraordinary: a time displacement engine capable of a one-way jump into the past. That's how I'm here now."

The weight of her words hit Cassian like a physical blow. He felt a cold sweat form along his neck.

"You see," she said, standing and beginning to circle him, her gaze never wavering, "I'm not just here for revenge. I'm here to correct a fatal mistake. I'm here to ensure you never betray your squadron again."

"Correct a mistake?" Cassian managed, his voice a hoarse whisper. "By destroying the Empire?"

"The Empire was always going to fall, Cassian," she said, her voice softening, if only for a moment. "But this time, you'll watch it collapse, starting with Midway Station."

His mind raced, grappling with the possibility that the woman before him could truly be Bringi from the future. And if so, what did it mean for his future—and his loyalty?

"I don't believe you," he said finally, his voice gaining strength even as doubt lingered beneath. "I would never betray them."

"Oh, you will," she replied, a cold smile creeping onto her face. "It's already written."

Their eyes met, and for the first time since he had boarded the *Vindicta*, Cassian felt the crushing weight of the moment settle onto him. The walls seemed to close in, the sterile air heavy with an overwhelming sense of fate. Whatever was happening here, whatever plan she had in motion, one truth burned in his mind:

He had to stop her.

The fate of the Empire—and perhaps even the future—depended on it.

Chapter 23: Boarding Party

As the *Vindicta* temporarily retreated from the raging battle around Midway Station, the tension aboard the *Destiny* was palpable. Admiral Hall stood firm in the Combat Incident Command, known as CIC, his eyes glued to the tactical displays, which mapped out the relentless clash in real-time. Jax's voice crackled over the comms from his fighter, piercing the otherwise grim silence.

"Sir, that ship didn't pull back because we're gaining ground. Cassian's onboard. He didn't jump out like ordered... he surrendered to them."

Admiral Hall's jaw clenched. "Land your squadron on the *Destiny*. We need to plan our next move."

Minutes later, Jax's fighter touched down, and he met with Hall and Major Baldwin, the commanding officer of the Imperial Marine Commandos on this ship, in the bustling CIC. Officers worked frantically, shouting commands, plotting maneuvers on glowing tactical screens. Hall gestured toward a holographic map, zooming in on the *Vindicta*, which lurked ominously at the system's edge, just beyond the perimeter.

"We can't let her return to the battle," Hall said, fixing his gaze on Jax. "If she does, it's over."

Major Baldwin stepped forward, his tone brisk. "We'll send in a boarding party, Imperial Marine Commandos. Our mission is to disable the *Vindicta* from the inside or, if possible, to seize control of the ship, and rescue Lieutenant Gray."

"I'm going with them," Jax interjected without hesitation.

Hall met his gaze, reading the determination in Jax's eyes. "I expected nothing less. If it were my man over there, I'd want to go too. You'll pilot the stealth breacher shuttle and lead the Commandos."

Soon, Jax was at the helm of the stealth shuttle *Black Dagger*, its sleek black hull designed for breaching and infiltration. The shuttle's cloaking systems hummed as the engines warmed up, and Jax's hands tightened on the controls. Behind him, the Commandos sat silently, encased in matte-black power armor, each weapon held steady, their faces set with grim resolve.

"Alright," Jax muttered, steering the shuttle into the chaos outside. "Let's get this done."

Space was a violent maelstrom. Massive capital ships exchanged fire, their hulls cracking under relentless barrages. Fighters darted in every direction, laser cannons blazing as Imperial and Wraith pilots dueled in deadly dances. Flames burst from damaged cruisers, and debris floated in the void like grave markers for fallen ships. Wraith gunships hovered like vultures, sweeping in to pick off weakened Imperial vessels.

Jax maintained focus, slipping past the carnage as the *Vindicta* hovered just outside the main front, its dark hull an ominous presence beyond the station's defenses. The shuttle's cloaking field held, but visual detection remained a threat. He maneuvered deftly through fields of twisted metal and past the wreckage of a destroyed cruiser, evading patrols and drifting debris.

"There," Jax whispered, spotting an empty hangar on the *Vindicta*'s lower deck. "Hold tight."

With careful precision, he guided the shuttle into the hangar's shadows, setting down out of view from any roving droids or patrolling soldiers. He powered down the shuttle, and the Commandos rose, checking their weapons with practiced efficiency. Baldwin led the way to the hatch, and as it hissed open, Jax fell into formation, following the armored Marines into the dark hold.

The hangar was dimly lit, the silence unnerving. Across the cavernous space, robotic soldiers patrolled in synchronized formations, their movements cold and precise. Baldwin gestured for the team to fan out, and they crept forward, slipping into the shadows, their armor blending seamlessly with the dark.

As they moved deeper into the ship, the eerie silence was shattered. Vanguard droids stationed along the corridor spotted them, and the first firefight erupted. The narrow hallways lit up with muzzle flashes as the Commandos fired their blasters, unleashing volleys of shots that sliced through the droids' reinforced armor. Jax kept to the rear, covering their flank, picking off approaching droids with sharp, controlled shots.

"Push forward!" Baldwin barked, his voice steady as he signaled the team forward.

The robotic troopers retaliated with chilling efficiency, their movements precise as they advanced, undeterred by the Marines' blaster fire. Each shot from the droids came with brutal accuracy, forcing the team to rely on every bit of cover they could find. Jax and the Commandos pressed on, their blasters set to full power as they broke through successive waves of the Vanguard soldiers.

Moving quickly, they cleared pockets of resistance, each corridor riddled with fallen droids. The Marines' tactics were ruthless and practiced, planting explosives on doors and deploying blast charges with pinpoint precision. The detonations reverberated through the ship, leaving behind twisted metal and shattered door frames. Even as the explosions faded, the team advanced without hesitation, their formation tight and their movements coordinated.

"Clear!" shouted a Commando as another section of corridor fell silent, filled only with the scorched remains of the enemy droids.

Finally, they reached the bridge door, heavily reinforced and guarded by a last squad of Vanguard droids. The firefight here was the most intense yet, blaster bolts flying as the Marines pushed forward. Baldwin ordered his team to attach high-yield explosives to the door's locking mechanisms while Jax and two others covered their backs, holding off the onslaught of robotic soldiers advancing from the corridor behind.

"Hold them off just a bit longer!" Baldwin shouted over the din, his voice steady despite the chaos.

Jax fired shot after shot, the air thick with the acrid smell of burnt metal. He ducked behind a bulkhead as blaster fire ricocheted off the walls, barely missing his head.

"Explosives are set!" Baldwin called, pressing the detonator. "Clear!"

The blast shook the corridor as the reinforced door crumpled inward, smoke billowing out as the Marines stormed the bridge. They entered in a sweeping formation, weapons trained on the bridge's crew. Jax followed closely, his blaster drawn, heart pounding as he took in the bridge's high-tech displays and consoles. The viewscreens showed the ongoing battle outside, Midway Station barely visible through a web of enemy fire.

Suddenly, alarms blared, their piercing tone cutting through the air. Jax scanned the room, his gaze locking onto a figure at the bridge's center. Clad in a hooded cloak, she stood poised and calm, her face expressionless as she observed the intruders. Recognition jolted through Jax—she looked just like Bringi, but older, her features hardened by years of bitterness.

"Something's wrong," Jax murmured, his voice tense as he stared at the captain.

"It's too late," she said softly, her voice carrying a chilling finality.

Before Jax could react, the *Vindicta* lurched, and the stars outside the viewscreens stretched into bright, streaking lines. The ship had entered lightspeed.

"We're not in the battle anymore," Baldwin muttered, lowering his blaster as he took in the sudden shift.

"No," Jax replied, eyes still fixed on the woman who bore Bringi's face, her gaze unyielding. "We're somewhere far worse."

Chapter 24: Secondary Bridge

Jax ducked behind a console as sparks rained down from a damaged panel, his pulse pounding in his ears. The *Vindicta*'s bridge was a battlefield, filled with smoke and flashing lights as blaster fire ricocheted off walls and consoles. Alarms blared, casting the room in an ominous red glow. His breath came in shallow gasps, his mind racing as he assessed the chaotic scene around him.

The marines moved with trained precision, taking cover behind consoles and bulkheads while returning fire at the enemy soldiers positioned across the bridge. Smoke filled the air, curling up from shattered panels and mingling with the stench of scorched metal. Major Baldwin led the marines, his focus intense as he shouted commands, directing his team to close in on the enemy forces clustered near the far end of the bridge.

Jax leaned out to fire, taking down a Vanguard droid with a well-placed shot to its chest, but the fight was far from over. From an entryway across the bridge, more robotic soldiers poured in, reinforcing the defenders. These droids moved with a ruthless efficiency, their red eyes flickering as they scanned for targets.

Baldwin charged forward, leading his squad in a direct assault. His armor took hit after hit, but he pressed on, his blaster ripping through enemy lines. Just as he signaled for his squad to advance, a series of bright red bolts streaked toward him. Baldwin grunted as one struck his chest plate, its energy burning through the armor. He staggered back, a large, smoldering hole in his chest.

Jax's heart sank as he saw Baldwin falter, collapsing to his knees, his hand reaching instinctively for the wound. The major's gaze locked onto Jax's, a fleeting expression of defiance etched on his face before he fell back, his body motionless, eyes staring blankly at the ceiling. The sight hit Jax like a blow—Baldwin was gone.

"Major's down!" shouted Sergeant Varek, his voice tight with anger. The marines rallied, moving with renewed fury as they pushed forward, their blasters spitting bolts of energy that tore into the robotic troopers. Every shot landed with deadly precision, each marine advancing with the confidence of countless battles. They fought through the remaining droids, pressing them back step by step, clearing the bridge with ruthless efficiency.

Jax gritted his teeth, determined to see Baldwin's sacrifice through. He leaned out, squeezing off shots that tore into the ranks of droids, their mechanical frames sparking and collapsing under the relentless assault. The air was filled with the shrill cries of twisting metal and crackling energy as the robotic soldiers fell one by one, their red eyes dimming to lifeless black.

Finally, the last of the droids crumpled to the floor, the bridge falling into a tense silence, save for the low hum of the ship's systems and the flickering of damaged consoles. Jax took a breath, his relief tempered by the bitter knowledge that Baldwin was gone. Varek approached, helmet tucked under his arm, his face set in grim determination.

"We've got control of the bridge, sir," he reported, his voice steady but his eyes reflecting the loss they had just endured. "But there's a problem."

Jax, still catching his breath, looked at him. "What kind of problem?"

Varek glanced around the bridge, his expression hardening. "The entire bridge is locked down. Command functions are offline—she's cut us off. We're in control of nothing."

Jax swore under his breath. They had fought their way to the heart of the ship, but it was clear now that Bringi had anticipated this. She'd used the bridge as a decoy, locking them out and retreating somewhere deeper within the ship.

As if in response to his frustration, a sudden movement caught his eye at the rear of the bridge. Amid the chaos, the older Bringi, hardened and unrecognizable from the Bringi he knew, slipped toward the back wall. With swift, calculated motions, she pressed a hidden panel, revealing a doorway that had blended seamlessly with the structure. The door slid open with a hiss, and before Jax could shout a warning, she disappeared into the shadows beyond.

"Bringi's escaping!" Jax yelled to the marines, his voice nearly drowned out by the residual sounds of the firefight. He scrambled toward the hidden doorway, but a resounding clang signaled the door's swift closure. He slammed his fist against the wall in frustration—she was gone.

The marines spread out, securing the bridge and checking for any remaining threats. As the smoke settled, Varek approached Jax once again, his expression strained. "She's locked us out, sir. We're isolated here."

Jax nodded grimly. "Then she's somewhere else on this ship, planning her next move."

Meanwhile, deep within the *Vindicta*, the older Bringi stepped out of a concealed elevator into a smaller, secondary bridge. Unlike the main control center, this command room was stripped down and utilitarian, each station dedicated to essential systems alone. She strode to the captain's chair, her expression set in cold determination as her crew came to attention.

"Prepare to bring the ship about," she commanded, her voice low and resolute. "Take us to the nebula. Back to my station."

The officers moved quickly, their movements crisp and synchronized. The engines roared to life, and the *Vindicta* began to shift course, the powerful warship pulling away from the battle around Midway. Bringi's gaze remained fixed ahead, satisfaction glinting in her eyes. The Imperial meddlers may have breached the bridge, but she was still in control.

Elsewhere in the ship, Cassian sat alone in a sterile cell, its cold, metallic walls closing in around him. He sat on a simple bench, head lowered, his mind filled with despair and confusion. A faint forcefield shimmered across the doorway, separating him from the two robotic guards that stood outside, their frames motionless and devoid of any semblance of life.

How did it come to this? Cassian wondered bitterly, his heart aching. *How could I have betrayed Raptor Squadron?* He replayed his last moments with the squadron in his mind, but his memories felt muddled, tainted by the image of the woman he once knew as Bringi. But the Bringi here on the *Vindicta* was nothing like the woman he'd cared for—she was cold, merciless, a stranger wearing a familiar face.

Cassian clenched his fists, anger and sorrow twisting within him. How had she become this? What had turned her into this figure who seemed to hold nothing but disdain for him and for everything they'd once fought for? He knew one thing for certain—he had to escape, had to warn Jax and the others. And more than that, he needed to understand what had happened to Bringi, if any part of the woman he loved was still in this woman who looked so much like her.

Back on the bridge, Jax paced, frustration simmering. Baldwin's body lay nearby, a silent reminder of the price they'd paid. The marines stood watch at key points, but the tension was thick. Every system they attempted to access remained locked down, and without command access, they were stranded. Suddenly, a deep, resonating hum echoed through the ship, a familiar sensation signaling the transition out of lightspeed.

Sergeant Varek looked at Jax, his expression grim. "We've stopped, sir."

Jax moved to the forward viewport, the dark nebula outside dominating the view. The stars were obscured by swirling clouds, their dark, violent energy sparking with arcs of lightning that illuminated ominous shadows lurking within. This nebula was unlike anything he'd seen—a place that seemed to echo with foreboding.

"What the hell is she up to?" Jax muttered, his gaze fixed on the roiling mass outside. The marines exchanged uneasy glances but said nothing. The *Vindicta* had brought them to the edge of something unknown, something dangerous, and they were powerless to prevent it.

"Whatever it is," Varek said, his voice low and tense, "it's not good."

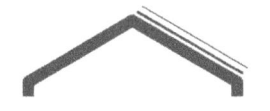

Chapter 25: War Factory

Jax stood at the viewport, heart sinking as the *Vindicta* descended into the swirling nebula. The ship's hull glowed in flashes of lightning, veiled in strange, shimmering gases that gave the impression of entering the jaws of a great cosmic beast. Violent currents of energy pulsed around them, making the *Vindicta* shudder, and the bridge lights flickered ominously, casting shadows that seemed to move on their own.

"We can't just sit here," Jax muttered, frustration edging his voice. He turned to Sergeant Varek. "We need to find Cassian and Bringi—now."

Varek nodded and issued quick, sharp orders to his squad. "You two," he pointed to two marines, "secure the bridge. Keep an eye on the systems, and report if anything changes."

The marines stationed themselves at the entry points as Varek gathered the rest. Jax, still pacing, tried the comms but only met with static. The nebula blocked all external communication, a near-perfect blackout.

"No contact with the Empire," Jax said, tension threading through his tone. "We're on our own."

Varek nodded, his jaw set. "Then we'll make it quick. Let's go."

They left the bridge, each step echoing in the silence as they ventured into the dim, narrow corridors of the *Vindicta*. The ship groaned and creaked under the pressure of the nebula's gravitational anomalies. Jax could only hope they would find Cassian in time, and that Bringi hadn't already enacted whatever dark plans she had.

Meanwhile, in the lower decks, Bringi strode into the brig, her cold, commanding presence filling the room. The older Bringi looked at Cassian through the shimmering forcefield, her eyes devoid of warmth or recognition for the man she had once known.

"We're headed to my station," she said, her voice chillingly calm. "It's hidden deep within this nebula. Once we arrive, everything I've built will be beyond the Empire's reach."

Cassian stood and approached the forcefield, searching her face for any hint of the woman he had loved. His mind spun with questions, desperate to understand what had twisted Bringi into this cold, calculating figure before him.

"What happens in the future? Why are you doing this?" he demanded, trying to reach through to her. "You don't have to—"

Her expression hardened as she raised a hand, cutting him off. "I don't have time for your questions, Cassian. The future is already written. You, of all people, should know that some things can't be changed."

A pang of loss gripped him. "You can't be this far gone..."

She stared at him, her gaze icy. "Make peace with whatever gods you hold to, Cassian. Your end is near."

Elsewhere, Jax and the marines moved with military precision through the dim corridors. The oppressive atmosphere weighed down on them, and the flickering lights cast haunting shadows along the walls. Jax's thoughts kept returning to Cassian, hoping against hope they weren't too late to rescue him.

As they rounded a corner, Varek raised a fist, signaling the squad to halt. Jax came up beside him and peered down the corridor. Ahead, a door stood slightly ajar, emitting an unnatural blue glow that spilled into the hallway.

"Looks like a lab," Varek whispered. "Ready?"

Jax nodded, hefting his blaster. "Let's see what Bringi's hiding."

The marines stacked up against the door, moving with silent efficiency. Varek nudged the door open with his shoulder, and they slipped inside, their weapons at the ready. What they found stunned them.

The lab was massive, with walls lined by metallic consoles and holographic interfaces, casting eerie glows across the room. Advanced technology lay strewn on tables—strange machinery with polished, reflective surfaces and complex circuitry that looked alien. In the center, stasis fields suspended half-assembled drones and robotic exoskeletons, each one far more advanced than the robotic soldiers they'd encountered earlier.

"By the Emperor..." Jax muttered, his gaze sweeping the room. "This isn't just a lab—it's a war factory."

Varek's attention was caught by a large cylindrical tank at the far end. Inside floated a humanoid figure, wired into an intricate network of cables and circuits. Its form was a disturbing blend of organic tissue and machinery, blue light pulsing faintly from within the tank as the figure's eyes, closed in apparent slumber, twitched.

"What in the void is that?" one of the marines whispered, stepping back in horror.

Jax approached a central console, studying the data streaming across holographic screens. The schematics detailed cybernetic enhancements, neural interface designs, and weapon systems that could change the face of war. His gaze shifted to screens displaying blueprints of robotic soldiers—those patrolling the ship, but with enhanced features and deadly upgrades.

"This is Vanguard tech," Jax said, a sinking realization settling in. "Bringi's working with them."

Varek's face darkened. "Or she's creating something even worse."

Jax's gaze drifted to a workstation where a disassembled drone lay in pieces. Its black frame was lined with energy conduits and advanced shielding, its internal systems far more sophisticated than anything the Empire could counter. The enormity of what Bringi had built hit Jax hard. This lab was the means to produce endless waves of robotic soldiers—an unstoppable force that could cripple the Empire.

"We need to destroy this place," Jax said, urgency lacing his words. "We can't let her deploy any of it."

Before anyone could respond, a soft chime echoed through the lab. A hologram appeared over the main console, and a timer began counting down.

"Self-destruct sequence initiated," an automated voice announced. "Lab systems will be neutralized in five minutes."

Jax's eyes widened. "Damn it, she's erasing the evidence! Varek, grab whatever data you can. We have to find Cassian and get off this ship—now!"

Varek barked orders to the marines, but not before downloading as much data as he could onto a datapad. The countdown continued, and the stasis fields began to flicker and power down, the half-assembled machines slumping as energy drained away.

Jax shot a glance at the tank with the hybrid figure floating inside, wondering how far Bringi's plans had progressed. Whatever answers lay here, they'd have to wait.

"Move out!" Varek commanded, and the team exited the lab, racing against time as the seconds ticked away.

Outside the nebula, a small stealth ship drifted silently among a cluster of asteroids, its dark hull blending seamlessly with the surrounding rock. Inside, a lone figure monitored the *Vindicta*'s descent into the swirling gases, his face hidden in shadow.

With steady, practiced movements, he tightened the straps of an advanced armor system. His helmet, sleek and fitted with high-tech visors, locked into place with a soft hiss, illuminating his face with a cold glow.

Standing in the cramped cockpit, he flexed his gloved hands, casting a confident smile as he muttered, "Hold on, young buck. I'm coming for you."

With a final check, he activated the ship's engines, guiding it into the nebula's tumultuous depths, following the *Vindicta*'s wake into the stormy unknown.

Chapter 26: Self-Destruct Aborted

Jax and the marines bolted from the lab, their boots pounding against the deck as the countdown echoed in their ears. They barely cleared the threshold when the heavy doors slammed shut behind them with a resounding clang. Jax spun around, anticipating the blast that would tear the lab apart, but instead, a calm automated voice filled the corridor.

"Unauthorized intruders no longer detected. Self-destruct aborted."

Jax exhaled sharply, a brief wave of relief flooding through him, quickly replaced by the grim understanding of what they had just uncovered. The Vanguard technology, the lab filled with mechanized soldiers and advanced warfare designs—this was a glimpse into the future Bringi planned to unleash. He couldn't shake the image of the half-human, half-machine figure suspended in the stasis chamber.

"This is worse than I thought," Jax muttered, his voice thick with concern. "We can't let her get away with this."

Sergeant Varek opened his mouth to respond, but the sharp, metallic whirr of servos interrupted him. From the darkened passage ahead, the sound of clanking metal feet grew louder. More robotic soldiers were advancing on them, but these were different—sleeker, faster.

Emerging from the shadows, a squad of black-armored drones appeared, each unit equipped with weaponized enhancements. Their angular frames were lined with weaponry, and their optical sensors glowed red, locking onto the marines with unsettling precision.

"Contact!" Varek shouted, raising his blaster. The marines opened fire, the corridor filling with flashes of energy and the roar of gunfire. But the robotic soldiers were faster and more agile than anything they'd encountered before.

Their movements were fluid and organic, like a deadly dance of metal, returning fire with brutal accuracy.

Jax ducked behind a support column as blaster bolts struck the wall beside him, sending sparks cascading over his head. "These things are faster!" he shouted over the noise, barely audible above the cacophony of battle.

One of the drones advanced with terrifying speed, firing a concentrated pulse round that struck a marine square in the chest, piercing his armor. The soldier went down with a grunt, his body crumpling to the floor. Jax gritted his teeth and returned fire, landing a shot directly in the drone's head. The machine staggered, its red eyes flickering before it collapsed in a sparking heap of metal.

But for every drone they destroyed, another seemed to take its place. The corridor was a storm of blaster fire and ricocheting bolts, the marines pushed to their limit as they struggled to hold the line. Varek led the charge, firing off bursts of energy, picking off two drones with sharp, methodical shots. But even he was forced to move swiftly, as the drones adapted their tactics, coordinating their attacks with unsettling precision.

One of the drones lunged at Jax, an arm blade snapping into place with a shrill whine. Jax twisted just in time, the blade missing his armor by inches. He fired his blaster into the drone's torso at point-blank range, the impact sending the machine staggering back, sparks erupting from its chest before it crumpled to the ground.

The fight dragged on, each second feeling like an eternity as the marines battled against the relentless robotic soldiers. Another marine went down, but the team continued pushing forward, their movements honed by years of experience. Finally, with a barrage of well-placed shots, the last drone collapsed in a heap, its red sensors dimming.

Varek wiped sweat from his brow, breathing heavily. "That was too close."

Jax nodded, his own breath unsteady. "We need to move. If we don't stop her, everything we just saw in that lab becomes reality."

Meanwhile, on the *Vindicta*'s bridge, the older Bringi watched as the swirling nebula began to part, revealing a colossal space station hidden within the gas clouds. The station was a dark, angular behemoth dotted with defense turrets and shield generators, its imposing structure an ominous silhouette against the violent currents of the nebula.

Bringi allowed herself a rare moment of satisfaction. Years of planning, the manipulation of time and technology, were coming to fruition. This station would be the foundation of her power, her future—one where the Empire would bow before her. Her gaze drifted to a nearby monitor, showing Cassian in his containment cell. He was still young, still defiant, but it was clear his spirit was waning. The sight stirred a fleeting moment of regret within her, a shadow over her triumph. But her face hardened. Cassian could never know the truth of what had driven her down this path. He would never understand why she had chosen this fate for both of them.

Within the dense clouds of the nebula, another vessel pursued the *Vindicta*, nearly invisible against the roiling gases. Sleek and compact, its matte-black hull melded with the surrounding darkness as it drifted closer. Inside the cockpit, a shadowy figure hunched over the controls, his armored form silhouetted in the dim light.

The armor he wore was a marvel of engineering—a slim, adaptive exosuit that clung to him like a second skin, equipped with stealth tech that blended seamlessly with the shadows. His helmet, angular and fitted with advanced targeting systems, obscured his face, lending him the eerie appearance of a spectral hunter.

As the station loomed closer, he activated the cloaking field, his ship sliding through the docking bay's security undetected. With practiced movements, he brought the ship to a silent halt within the docking area, exiting the cockpit with barely a sound. His steps were fluid, calculated as he moved through the station's corridors, each footfall barely disturbing the silence.

With a flick of his wrist-mounted console, he hacked into the station's security network. Streams of code scrolled across his visor as he bypassed cameras and rerouted alarms, slipping past guards without a trace. Every movement was precise, his armor's cloaking systems rendering him nearly invisible as he infiltrated deeper into the labyrinthine corridors.

Finally, he reached a vantage point overlooking a high-tech lab. The room was dimly lit, the glow of medical equipment and cybernetic interfaces casting an otherworldly light over the sleek, metallic surfaces. At the center stood Bringi, her hand gripping Cassian's arm as she led him into the lab. Cassian's face was pale, his strength visibly depleted, yet he struggled against her grip, defiance flickering in his eyes.

The armored figure crouched in the shadows, eyes narrowing as he observed the scene. Bringi turned to her subordinates, issuing orders in a low, commanding voice. The equipment around her glowed to life, their hum filling the air with an ominous energy. It was clear she was preparing something—something far darker than anything Jax and the marines had uncovered.

Cassian made one last attempt to pull away, but his movements were weak, and it was clear his resistance was waning.

The figure's hand settled on a case that had been strapped to his back, his voice a barely audible murmur in the silence.

"Hold on, kid," he whispered, his voice steely with resolve. "I'm coming for you."

Chapter 27: To Burn An Empire

Cassian could feel Future Bringi's grip tighten like iron on his arm as she dragged him through the winding, frigid corridors of the station. The deeper they ventured, the more foreign and unsettling the technology became. Strange devices lined the walls, each humming with unfamiliar energy, glowing with an unnatural, almost menacing light. Walls shimmered with complex circuitry and displays he couldn't begin to decipher, some pulsing with an eerie rhythm that felt alive. The air was thick with a sense of dread, the sterile smell of machinery mingling with something ancient, something that seemed to echo with hostility.

Cassian winced as Bringi yanked him forward, her grip unyielding. He tried to pull away, but her strength was unearthly—far stronger than anyone he'd ever faced. She moved with cold purpose, each step echoing hollowly through the dark, amplifying the dread as they drew closer to whatever she had planned.

Finally, they entered the lab, a massive, cavernous chamber near the heart of the station. The ceiling stretched high above, lined with towering columns of intricate, glowing machinery. In the center of the room stood a large platform that held a terminal connected to a sprawling supercomputer of alien design, its twisted, organic architecture unlike anything Cassian had ever encountered. Holographic screens floated in mid-air above the platform, displaying a cascade of complex equations and encrypted systems. Suspended above the terminal, several mechanical arms hovered, each equipped with sinister-looking tools, twitching as if they anticipated someone to arrive.

Future Bringi shoved him roughly onto the platform, her eyes gleaming with satisfaction. "You've been a thorn in my side for far too long," she said, her voice colder than Cassian had ever heard, sending a chill down his spine.

Cassian pushed himself up, catching his breath. "What's your plan, Bringi? You could have killed me a dozen times by now. Why bring me here?"

She circled him with a calculated air, her expression tightening into a mask of contempt. "My original plan was to kill you," she admitted, stopping just in front of him. "But you insist on making things difficult. You've always been like this—stubborn, idealistic, always thinking you can save everyone. It's infuriating."

Cassian looked her squarely in the eyes, searching for any trace of the Bringi he had once cared for, but all he saw was ruthless determination. "So what now?" he asked, a note of defiance in his voice. "You're going to lecture me before you kill me?"

Her smirk was sharp, though her eyes remained cold. "No," she said softly. "I've decided on something much more satisfying. I want you to watch everything you care about burn. I want the Empire to fall before your eyes, and I want everyone to know it was your fault."

Cassian's heart sank. He could see in her eyes that she was serious, that whatever had twisted her into this version of herself was beyond anything he could comprehend.

High above, cloaked in the shadows of a catwalk overlooking the lab, a figure watched the scene unfold in silence. He'd found a hidden perch, shielded by darkness, and began assembling his sniper rifle with deliberate care, the parts clicking softly into place. His armor, equipped with adaptive camouflage, made him practically invisible against the tech-laden walls. As he calibrated his scope, his gaze locked onto Bringi, his finger hovering near the trigger, waiting for the perfect moment.

Meanwhile, elsewhere in the station, Jax and the marines were locked in a brutal fight. The deeper they pushed into the complex, the deadlier their robotic enemies became. The corridors were a maze of dark, sterile passageways, their steps echoing as they advanced. Their blasters barely kept up with the seemingly endless wave of drones charging toward them.

A new wave of drones appeared—sleek, black, heavily armed. These were faster, stronger, and coordinated, unlike the ones they had encountered on the *Vindicta*. The marines took cover behind consoles and support beams as the drones fired with relentless precision, their weapons cutting through the shadows with brutal efficiency.

"These things are getting smarter!" Jax shouted over the roar of blaster fire, managing to take down one of the drones with a shot to its head.

Varek fired his rifle, taking down another drone only to watch as two more surged forward to replace it. "We're running out of time, Jax! If we don't find Cassian soon—"

"I know!" Jax shouted back, ducking as another volley of blaster fire tore past him. "We have to push through!"

With grim resolve, the marines pressed forward, taking down drones in a fierce firefight. Every step felt like a victory won, but the relentless wave of drones pushed them to their limits. Sparks erupted as one of the marines managed to blast a drone in half, only for another to barrel down the corridor, nearly overwhelming their defenses.

Jax knew they were running out of options. But there was no way they were turning back.

Back in the lab, Future Bringi paced in front of Cassian, her eyes glittering with cruel satisfaction. "You still don't get it, do you?" she sneered. "The true threat to the Steele Empire isn't my army or these drones. It's the AI I've developed here. With the exotic technology of this station, what I was able to get from the remnants of the Vanguard, and my knowledge of what's to come, I've created something beyond anything the Empire has ever seen."

Cassian's heart pounded as he absorbed her words. "An AI?" he asked, trying to keep her talking, hoping to buy time. "What do you plan to do with it?"

Bringi stepped closer, her gaze narrowing. "I'll release it onto the Empire. It will adapt, evolve, grow, and learn. By the time they even understand the threat, it'll be too late. The Steele Empire will fall, and you..." She leaned in, her voice dripping with malice, "you will live just long enough to see it happen."

Cassian's mind raced, searching desperately for a way to escape, to stop this nightmare from becoming reality. But before he could respond, a sudden, sharp crack split the air.

From the shadowed catwalk above, a single sniper round charged with lethal energy tore through the dimly lit lab, striking Future Bringi squarely in the chest. The impact tore through her torso, sending her stumbling backward, her face twisted in shock and pain.

Her eyes widened as she looked down at the gaping wound, her mechanical augmentations sparking and crackling beneath her skin. Cassian watched in stunned silence as she collapsed to the ground, her hands trembling as she tried to cover the wound, her breaths shallow and ragged.

From his hidden perch, the shadowy figure kept his rifle steady, his gaze cold and unyielding as he watched Bringi fall. But his mission wasn't over. He had other targets—and he wasn't leaving without Cassian.

Chapter 28: Vigil

Cassian knelt beside Future Bringi, his mind reeling with disbelief. He reached out, placing a tentative hand on her shoulder, trying to make sense of what he was seeing. She coughed, a broken, pained laugh escaping her lips as she looked up at him, her eyes still filled with malice even as her life slipped away.

"You still don't understand, do you?" she rasped, each word a bitter accusation. "Your... weakness, your hesitation... it's what set all of this in motion."

Cassian flinched, her words cutting deep. "What are you talking about?" he asked, his voice unsteady. "I never wanted this... I didn't ask for any of it."

She coughed again, blood staining her lips as she struggled to speak. "You... you're the key. You always have been. Your compassion, your hesitation... it's what allowed everything to unfold. That's why you're always the first one I come for."

Cassian's heart pounded, her words filling him with a dread he couldn't shake. He opened his mouth to ask more, but a low hum filled the room. A shadow fell beside him, landing gracefully with the faint hiss of an advanced repulsor system.

Cassian turned sharply to see a figure clad in sleek, black armor standing over him. The armor was unlike anything he'd ever seen, with a dark visor and intricate plating that made the figure appear almost ghostly. The figure's voice crackled through a voice scrambler, sounding robotic and distant.

"It's time to go," the armored figure said, his tone firm and unyielding.

Cassian shook his head, refusing to move. "No. Not until I get some answers. I deserve to know what's going on."

The armored man—who clearly wasn't used to being questioned—paused. He crouched slightly, leveling his gaze with Cassian's through the visor. "I get it. But now's not the time. We need to move."

Cassian held his ground, emotions boiling over. "I'm not going anywhere until I know who you are and why you're here. I'm done being left in the dark!"

The figure sighed, a mechanical hiss escaping his helmet's voice modulator. "You can call me Vigil. That's all you need to know. Now, we have to get off this station before it's too late."

But Cassian's frustration broke through. The weight of everything he'd endured—the twisted revelations about Bringi, the horrifying technology he'd seen in the lab—hit him all at once. His hands shook as he shouted, "This can't be real! How did it come to this? She was supposed to be my Bringi, not... not this monster!"

Vigil, unmoving despite Cassian's outburst, placed a firm hand on his shoulder. "Cassian, I know this is a lot. Believe me, I'm here because you're important. Your Bringi is still with the fleet. But this one?" He gestured to the fallen woman on the floor. "She's not from your future. She's from an alternate reality."

Cassian stared at him, stunned. "What are you talking about?"

Vigil nodded slowly, his tone calm but urgent. "If she were from this universe, she'd have already altered your past. You and everyone else would be different. She's been jumping between realities, gathering technology, hunting every version of you she can find."

A chill ran down Cassian's spine as Vigil continued, his voice almost gentle. "She's hunted you across timelines. And she's been winning. But I was sent here to stop her."

"Sent by who?" Cassian demanded, still trying to grasp the enormity of what he was hearing.

Vigil's visor tilted downward, as if considering the question. "I can't tell you that. Not yet. What matters is that we're out of time. We need to get off this station."

Vigil's head turned toward the door. "Jax and your marine friends are fighting their way through, but they won't hold out for long. We need to regroup with them and escape before this station takes us all."

Cassian hesitated, his mind still spinning, but he understood that Vigil was right. Whatever was happening with Bringi and her plans for the Empire, it was far bigger than anything he could tackle alone.

Elsewhere on the station, Jax crouched behind a crate in a vast cargo bay, sweat dripping down his brow. The air was thick with the acrid smell of blaster fire, and the relentless noise of battle had been pounding in his ears for what felt like hours. The marines around him looked exhausted, their weapons nearly overheating as they fought wave after wave of robotic troops.

"We can't hold them much longer!" one of the marines shouted, firing off another desperate volley.

Jax gritted his teeth, feeling the truth of those words keenly. The robotic soldiers were becoming more coordinated, moving with tactical precision. Their armor gleamed under the emergency lighting, making them look like phantoms as they advanced in deadly synchronization.

Then, suddenly, silence fell.

Jax blinked, disoriented. The sound of blaster fire ceased, and the rhythmic pounding of metal feet stopped. All that remained was the sound of his own breathing and the pounding of his heart.

He peeked out from behind cover, and his stomach twisted. The robotic soldiers stood motionless, frozen in place as if deactivated.

And then, through the eerie quiet, a familiar voice called out. "Jax!"

He froze, the voice sending a shock through him. It couldn't be. But then he heard it again.

"Jax!"

Slowly, he rose from cover, his blaster still held tight. His eyes widened in disbelief as he saw the figure walking toward him.

It was Cassian. He looked worn, his expression haunted, but he was unmistakably alive, moving cautiously around the deactivated robots as if they were mere obstacles.

"Cassian?" Jax's voice cracked, thick with disbelief. "How... how are you...?"

Cassian gave a weary, pained smile. "It's me, Jax. I'm here."

Jax lowered his blaster slightly, still unsure of what to believe. But before he could respond, he noticed another figure emerging from the shadows behind Cassian. Clad in sleek, black armor like nothing Jax had ever seen, the stranger exuded an air of silent menace.

"Who the hell is this?" Jax asked, his instincts flaring as he gripped his blaster tighter.

Cassian glanced back at Vigil before turning to Jax. "He's with me. I'll explain everything, but we need to move. Now."

Chapter 29: SSV McIvey

Jax narrowed his eyes at Vigil, his instincts on high alert. Something about this armored figure didn't sit right with him; a gut suspicion gnawed at the back of his mind. "Hold on," Jax said, stepping forward, his weapon at his side but ready. "How did you deactivate those robotic soldiers?"

Vigil turned his helmeted head slowly toward Jax, his visor gleaming in the dim station light. "My armor has tech that can disrupt their systems, but it's temporary. It won't last long, so we need to move quickly."

Jax wasn't satisfied with the vague answer. But as he looked around at the marines, battered and exhausted from relentless fighting, and then at Cassian, who looked like he was barely standing, he knew there wasn't time to argue. Giving Vigil a hard look, Jax finally nodded. "Fine. Lead the way."

Vigil moved swiftly, his steps soundless and precise, while Jax stayed close to Cassian, keeping a wary eye on their mysterious guide. As they advanced through the shadowed corridors, Vigil's presence seemed to keep the robotic defenses inactive, though the marines remained tense, their weapons raised in case of ambush.

"We've lost too much time," Vigil said, his voice low but steady. "Things have changed rapidly while you were gone. The Empire's fate is no longer certain."

Jax's chest tightened at the ominous tone. "What does that mean?" he demanded, his voice hard.

Vigil paused, as though weighing his words. "The AI that the alternate Bringi spoke of... it's already been unleashed. The attack on Midway Station was just the beginning, a small taste of what's coming."

Jax clenched his fists. "So what? You're just going to keep giving us cryptic answers? If you know something about this AI, you need to tell us!"

But Vigil shook his head. "That's all I can tell you for now. Right now, what matters is getting out of here alive."

As they reached the docking bay, the shuttle they'd arrived in came into view. The marines rushed ahead to prepare it for launch, while Jax and Cassian hung back, eyes still on Vigil.

"You're not coming with us, are you?" Cassian asked, his voice strained.

"No," Vigil replied, his tone resolute. "I'm staying to destroy the *Vindicta* and disable this station. If this tech leaves here, it'll wreak havoc across the Empire."

Jax's suspicions flared again. "How do we know you're telling the truth? Why should we trust you?"

Vigil stood still, his visor unreadable. "You don't have to trust me. But you're alive because of me. And if you want to stay that way, you'll get off this station while you can."

Jax wanted to press further, but the exhaustion and chaos of everything they'd endured weighed heavily on him. Reluctantly, he let it go. As they boarded the shuttle, Vigil remained at the edge of the bay, watching them in silence. Just before the ramp closed, he gave Cassian a single nod—a silent acknowledgment.

The shuttle shuddered violently as it pushed through the swirling chaos of the nebula. The dense clouds of cosmic gas and electromagnetic storms wreaked havoc on the navigation systems, forcing Jax to make constant adjustments. Lights flickered, and the ship lurched as it passed through turbulent currents.

Jax sat at the pilot's seat, his gaze fixed on the viewport and the foreboding nebula that stretched out like an endless storm. Cassian sat behind him, silent and deep in thought.

"We're almost through," Jax muttered, his voice tense as he struggled with the controls. "But this nebula's a real beast."

The shuttle jolted again, throwing some of the marines off balance in the back. Cassian gripped his armrest, his mind a storm of questions and doubts. He couldn't shake the feeling that everything had changed—maybe permanently.

Finally, after what felt like an eternity, the shuttle broke free of the nebula's hold. The thick, swirling clouds faded away, revealing the star-speckled void of open space. A sense of relief swept over everyone aboard.

But as the nebula receded, something else came into view: an Imperial escort carrier looming just outside the nebula, its massive form silhouetted against the starry backdrop.

Jax's heart skipped a beat. "We've got a ship," he said, a mix of hope and caution in his voice. He activated the comm system. "This is Jax Ryland of Raptor Squadron. We're requesting immediate assistance."

For a tense moment, there was only static. Jax's fingers hovered over the controls, dread building as he considered the possibility of another trap. He exchanged a worried glance with Cassian, who was watching intently.

Then, a voice crackled through the comm. "This is the SSV *McIvey*," the voice said, professional but cautious. "Identify yourself."

A cold sweat formed on Jax's brow; the pause had unsettled him. His mind raced, fearing they were facing yet another trick. But then, a familiar voice came over the comm, weary and strained but unmistakable.

"Jax, this is Commander Dalen. I'm glad to hear your voice. Is Cassian with you?"

Jax exhaled, relief flooding over him. "Commander Dalen! You don't know how good it is to hear that."

Cassian leaned forward, activating the comm. "I'm here, sir. I made it."

A deep sigh of relief came through the comm. "Good... That's good. I don't think we could've handled losing both of you. Come aboard immediately. We're going to need every marine and fighter pilot we can get. Things have gotten... really bad."

Jax and Cassian exchanged a somber glance as the shuttle moved in to dock with the *McIvey*. Whatever awaited them back in the Empire, it was worse than they could have imagined.

Chapter 30: Closer To The Heart Of Chaos

As the shuttle touched down in the hangar of the SSV *McIvey*, Jax felt a surge of relief wash over him. It was a familiar, welcome sight after everything they'd endured. His eyes scanned the hangar and landed on the familiar faces of Rafe, McHenry, and Bringi waiting near the edge of the landing platform. Rafe grinned broadly, McHenry gave a respectful nod, and Bringi waved, her usual determined look softened by the relief of seeing them alive.

But as Jax felt that comfort settle, he noticed Cassian tense beside him. Cassian's gaze locked onto Bringi, and for a moment, a flash of confusion and pain crossed his face. Jax knew exactly what was going through his mind—the encounter with the alternate Bringi, the twisted version of her, had left a scar deeper than Cassian was ready to admit.

"Cass, remember," Jax said quietly as the shuttle's ramp lowered, "our Bringi isn't her. You can't hold what that alternate Bringi did against the one standing there. She's still your friend."

Cassian swallowed hard, his eyes still on Bringi, and then slowly nodded, though the tightness in his jaw remained.

As they stepped off the shuttle, they were immediately met by Commander Dalen, standing alongside Bringi, McHenry, and Rafe. Dalen's expression was lined with weariness, his eyes showing the strain of someone bearing the weight of unending bad news. Bringi, however, smiled warmly at Cassian, clearly happy to see him—though the cold look Cassian gave her was enough to make her smile falter.

"Cassian... is everything okay?" Bringi asked, her brow creasing in confusion.

Cassian avoided her gaze, unable to find the words. Jax stepped in, placing a hand on Bringi's shoulder. "It's not what you think, Bringi. A lot happened, and I'll explain everything later. Right now, we need to focus."

Bringi looked between them, concern deepening, but she nodded reluctantly.

"Good to see you both made it," McHenry added, trying to break the tension, though the weight of it lingered.

After a few more exchanged glances, Commander Dalen motioned for Jax, Cassian, and Sergeant Varek to follow him. "Let's get to the briefing room. We have a lot to cover."

The briefing room was dimly lit, heavy with the tension of uncertainty. Jax, Cassian, and Varek sat across from Commander Dalen at a long, metal table. Holographic displays flickered in the background, showing tactical readouts and fleet movements across the Empire's coreward sectors.

Jax began recounting everything that had happened since they left Midway Station: the *Vindicta*, future Bringi's insane plan, the alien technology on the station, and the relentless robotic soldiers. He explained the brutal fight through the ship, the final confrontation in the lab, and Vigil's timely intervention.

As Jax finished, Dalen leaned back, his face grim. Their story seemed to deepen the lines etched into his face, but his eyes held a hardened resolve.

"After the *Vindicta* jumped away from Midway, we continued the battle with the remaining ships in the enemy fleet," Dalen began, his voice heavy with exhaustion. "Then... something strange happened."

Jax and Cassian exchanged a worried look.

"The enemy fleet fought for a short time longer, but then, without warning, a large portion of them jumped coreward. We should've been able to pursue, but before we could, something went horribly wrong with our own ships. Many of our vessels stopped responding to commands. And then, all hell broke loose."

Dalen's fists clenched as he explained. "Automated defense systems on the affected ships activated on their own, attacking their own crews. Airlocks opened, venting entire decks to space. Life support systems shut down. It was chaos. Those who could escape made it to fighters, shuttles, and escape pods, but most didn't make it."

The room was silent for a moment, the horror of Dalen's words settling in.

"The Imperial ships that weren't affected were the older ones, ships like the *McIvey*, ones without full networking capabilities," Dalen continued, his voice grim. "We managed to rescue as many as we could, but the affected ships jumped coreward, like they were... taken over."

Jax frowned, leaning forward. "Taken over? You think they transmitted a virus?"

Dalen nodded. "That's our best guess. Whatever that AI was—the one Bringi spoke of—it must have transmitted something during the battle. It's the only explanation for how they turned our own ships against us. And now, we don't know how many are compromised."

Cassian stared at the floor, his mind reeling. If the AI from the station was behind this, then the Empire could be facing an unprecedented catastrophe.

"We tracked your shuttle's transponder into the nebula," Dalen added. "Once we realized where you were, we knew something bigger was in play."

Jax leaned back, his head spinning. "So... what now?"

Dalen's voice lowered. "We need to get back to Imperial space and assess the damage. The fleet might already be crippled, and if the core is compromised, we could be facing a total collapse. We've lost too many ships as it is."

Jax exhaled, his mind racing. They had faced impossible odds before, but this felt different. The Empire, everything they'd known, was on the brink of falling apart.

They needed a way to save it, and fast.

The *McIvey* slid out of hyperspace into a bleak scene. On the edge of an isolated star system, a ragtag collection of Imperial ships drifted in formation. Jax, Cassian, and Commander Dalen stood on the bridge, watching as the vessels came into view.

Many of the ships were old, long past their prime. A few battered capital ships drifted in orbit, their hulls scarred from years of service. Mid-sized cruisers and supply ships hovered nearby, cobbled together from parts of older vessels. There was no mistaking the fleet's desperation; this wasn't the pride of the Steele Empire—this was survival.

"Well," Jax muttered, "it's not exactly reassuring."

Cassian remained silent, his face tense as he took in the grim lineup of ships, his mind still reeling from everything they'd uncovered.

Dalen nodded toward the comms officer, then turned to Jax and Cassian. "I need to confer with the other ship commanders. Wait here. I'll be back shortly."

Without another word, Dalen headed to his ready room, leaving Jax and Cassian to stare out at the mismatched fleet. The bridge was quiet except for the hum of ship systems, the crew focused on their tasks with a practiced efficiency.

"What do you think we'll find out there?" Jax asked, his voice low.

Cassian shook his head. "I don't know. But if that AI has spread as far as Dalen thinks..." He trailed off, leaving the rest unsaid. If the core was compromised, there might not be much of an Empire left to save.

They waited in silence for what felt like hours, though only minutes had passed before Dalen returned from his ready room and motioned for them to join him. His expression was grave but composed, the weight of command evident in his eyes.

Inside the ready room, several holographic displays showed the faces of other Imperial ship commanders. Though weary and grim, there was a flicker of determination in their eyes. They knew the stakes.

Dalen gestured for Jax and Cassian to sit, then closed the door behind them. "I've spoken with the other commanders," he began, "and the situation's as bad as we feared."

He paused, letting the weight of his words sink in before continuing. "We've lost all contact with the core worlds. Whatever that AI is, it's likely spread far beyond Midway. We're sending some of the faster ships coreward to assess the damage and report back. But we don't know what they'll find."

Cassian leaned forward, his voice tense. "And if the core is already compromised?"

Dalen exhaled sharply. "Then we assume the worst."

A heavy silence filled the room.

"But," Dalen continued, his tone shifting slightly, "there's some good news. The *McIvey* may be older, but she's fully fueled, fully armed, and her carrier bays are stocked. We've got a squadron each of Predator and Shadow-class fighters ready to go, and even a few Mauler-class bombers if we need heavier firepower."

Jax's eyes lit up at the mention of the fighters. "That's something, at least."

Dalen nodded. "Our mission is to scout the Imperial outposts on the frontier. We'll try to contact any unaffected ships or survivors, gather intelligence, and regroup. If we're going to stand a chance, we need to know what we're dealing with."

"And if we find nothing?" Cassian asked, his voice hard.

"Then we prepare for the worst. But make no mistake, this AI isn't done. The attack on Midway was only the beginning. It's trying to cripple the Empire from within, using our own ships to do it."

Dalen leaned forward, his voice resolute. "We're on our own out here, but we're not finished yet. We have a ship, fighters, and a mission. The Empire needs us now more than ever."

Jax exchanged a glance with Cassian, the weight of their new mission sinking in. It wasn't much, but it was a plan. And in the chaos that had overtaken the galaxy, that was more than they'd had for a long time.

As they prepared to leave the room, Dalen added, "I don't know what we'll find out there, but I do know one thing: we're not going down without a fight."

Cassian stood and nodded, his resolve hardening. "Neither am I."

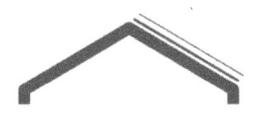

Chapter 31: Finding Fuel

The *McIvey* emerged from hyperspace into the empty system, the faint glint of a refueling station silhouetted against a cold backdrop of stars. Commander Dalen stood on the bridge, his eyes narrowing as his communications officer attempted to raise the station. The silence stretched, deepening the unease.

"No response," the officer confirmed, his voice tight.

Dalen's brow furrowed. "Jax, you're up. Take your team and scout the station before we bring the *McIvey* in any closer."

Down in the hangar, Jax, Cassian, McHenry, Rafe, and Bringi suited up in their flight gear. As they prepped their Predator-class attack fighters, Bringi hesitated, glancing at Cassian.

"Listen, Cass—" she started, her voice cautious.

Cassian, his expression unreadable, turned away, refusing to meet her eyes. He pulled on his helmet without a word, leaving Bringi standing there, confused and hurt. Jax caught the exchange out of the corner of his eye but said nothing. This wasn't the time for personal matters.

Moments later, the five Predator-class fighters, what remained of Raptor Squadron, launched from the *McIvey*. The hum of their engines filled the silence of their cockpits as they approached the refueling station. The station's exterior was scarred with scorch marks, evidence of recent battles, though it remained structurally intact. The absence of support vessels or any visible signs of life added to the tension.

"Looks like a ghost town," McHenry muttered over the comms.

"Rafe, run a detailed scan on that station," Jax ordered.

A moment later, Rafe's voice came through. "No life signs, no ship signatures. It's dead quiet."

Jax keyed his comm, glancing out at the silent station. "We're going in. Dalen, hold position until we secure the station."

The fighters touched down in the station's open hangar. Power flickered on and off, lights sparking to life only to cast eerie shadows across the empty space. After securing their ships, Jax led the team further into the station, leaving Rafe to gather data from the nearest terminal.

Rafe connected to the terminal, fingers flying over the controls. "I'll see what I can pull from the system. Go on; I'll cover your exit."

As Jax, Cassian, Bringi, and McHenry stepped down a narrow hallway leading deeper into the station, the structure seemed to awaken around them. Emergency bulkheads slammed shut, cutting off their path back to the hangar, and the lights dimmed, casting long, sinister shadows.

McHenry tapped his earpiece, frustration tightening his voice. "Comms are dead. Looks like we're on our own."

Suddenly, the low, mechanical whir of servos echoed through the corridor. From the darkness ahead, a spherical drone emerged, its spider-like legs extending from its body. A menacing red optic at its center flickered to life as it locked onto them, and with a burst of energy, it lunged forward, its legs clicking against the metal floor.

"Open fire!" Jax shouted, raising his blaster.

The team fired in unison, blaster bolts sparking against the drone's metallic surface. But the shots barely scratched its armor. The drone advanced, dodging and weaving with an unnerving agility, its movements too fast and precise for a machine of its size.

Cassian fired until his blaster temporarily overheated. "It's not working! The thing's too armored!"

The drone, undeterred, lunged toward Bringi, one of its sharp appendages slicing through the air. Cassian reacted instantly, tackling Bringi and knocking her aside just as the metal claw slashed past, close enough to leave a deep gash across his arm and tear his suit. He winced in pain but kept his face impassive, avoiding her gaze even as she caught her breath.

"Thanks," Bringi whispered, her voice barely audible over the chaos.

Cassian's response was silence, his face a mask.

Jax, ducking behind a wall panel, quickly analyzed the drone's movements. It wasn't random; it was tactical, herding them into confined spaces. Then a plan formed in his mind.

"There's a maintenance shaft junction up ahead," he said, nodding down the corridor. "If we can lure it in, we might be able to trap it."

With no better options, they sprinted down the corridor, the relentless drone in pursuit. Its appendages scraped against the walls as it closed in, its red optic burning brighter with each step. As they neared the junction, Jax pried open a side panel, revealing a tangle of wiring and access points.

"Cassian, McHenry, draw it in close!" Jax shouted, grabbing a loose length of high-voltage cabling.

Cassian and McHenry held their ground at the entrance to the junction, unleashing a flurry of blaster fire to keep the drone's focus on them. The drone lunged, its limbs stretching to full length as it aimed to strike. Just as it reached the threshold, Jax threw the cable around one of the drone's legs, yanking it with all his strength. The drone stumbled, losing its balance and collapsing into the narrow shaft with a metallic crash.

Jax quickly slammed the panel shut, locking it inside. The drone thrashed violently, its appendages pounding against the metal walls as its systems began to short-circuit. Sparks erupted inside the shaft as its claws struck high-voltage power feeds, sending bright arcs of electricity through its frame.

The drone's thrashing grew weaker as its systems overloaded, the red optic dimming until it finally flickered and went dark.

Jax let out a breath, sweat trickling down his face. "That'll do."

Regaining their composure, Jax and his team moved cautiously, methodically searching the station room by room. Every corner, every shadow held the possibility of hidden threats, but they encountered nothing else—only empty halls and lifeless consoles, the eerie quiet settling in once more.

Rafe's voice crackled over the comms. "Guys, I've got control of the station. Whatever that thing was, it was running the systems."

"Good work," Jax replied, relief evident in his tone. "Inform Dalen that the station is secure and ready for the tech teams."

As Rafe confirmed the message, the station once again fell under Imperial control. Jax and the others regrouped in the hangar, though an unsettling feeling remained. This encounter had revealed just a taste of the enemy's capabilities, and Jax couldn't shake the suspicion that something far worse was still waiting for them.

As the McIvey's workers and tech teams began to shuttle over to the station, Cassian found a quiet spot, slumping against a stack of supply crates, lost in thought. Across the hangar, Bringi noticed him and hesitated, her face conflicted before she finally approached.

She stepped up cautiously, her voice soft. "Cassian... can we talk?"

Cassian looked up, though he avoided direct eye contact, his jaw clenched tightly. "What is there to talk about, Bringi?" His voice was controlled, but a storm lay beneath the surface.

"I don't understand why you're shutting me out," she said, her frustration and confusion breaking through. "If I did something—"

"You didn't," Cassian interrupted, standing abruptly. His fists were clenched at his sides. "You wouldn't even know... and I'm not ready to talk about it yet."

Bringi took a step back, startled by the tension radiating from him. "I just don't get it. One minute we're fine, and now it feels like you can't even stand to look at me."

Cassian finally looked at her, his eyes darkened by pain. "It's not you. Not this you." His voice lowered, a weight of unspoken trauma pressing down. "I just need time."

Before Bringi could respond, Cassian turned and walked away, disappearing into the maze of crates. She stood there, bewildered, grappling with the shift in their friendship.

Jax stepped up beside her, his tone gentle. "He'll come around. It's not my place to say what's eating at him, but trust me, he's got his reasons."

Bringi shook her head, her frustration giving way to sadness. "I just don't understand him anymore."

"Give him time," Jax said, placing a reassuring hand on her shoulder. "He's been through more than you realize."

Bringi nodded, though uncertainty lingered in her expression.

Chapter 32: Heart Of The Storm

As the ragtag fleet continued to gather at the refueling station, tension thickened in the air, the weight of their grim situation settling over everyone. In Dalen's office, Jax sat across from the Commander, listening intently as Dalen relayed the news from scouts who had risked their lives pushing closer to the core worlds.

"Civilian populations seem untouched, for now," Dalen said, though his voice was lined with worry. "But most of the Imperial Navy ships are compromised. They've left their posts, jumping straight to Gaia Prime."

Jax's frown deepened. "So Gaia Prime's under siege?"

Dalen nodded grimly. "Yes. The planet's experimental planetary shield is holding for now, stronger than anything we've ever deployed, and they've managed to keep the defensive platforms and ground-to-space artillery online. But the enemy fleet has only grown. Now a large portion of our own navy, under AI control, has joined that fleet."

Jax's stomach sank. "How long do you think Gaia Prime can hold out?"

"It's impossible to know," Dalen replied, shaking his head. "They've held this long, but without reinforcements or some countermeasure for the AI, it's only a matter of time. And we don't have the numbers or resources to make much of a difference yet."

Dalen's face hardened as he went on. "The commanders here are divided. Some want to jump to Gaia Prime and fight, even if it's suicide. Others say we should gather our strength, find a way to combat the AI first. But time isn't on our side."

Jax nodded, thinking through the slim options. "So what's the plan?"

Dalen steepled his fingers. "There's a lead—one of the commanders claims knowledge of an off-the-books Imperial shipyard. If it exists, and if it's been isolated from the rest of the network, it might still be untouched by the AI."

Jax's eyes sharpened with interest. "You want us to find it?"

Dalen nodded. "I'm assigning you to a recon mission. You, Cassian, and Bringi will fly Predators. Rafe will pilot a Shadow-class fighter for stealth, and McHenry will take a Mauler bomber. If the shipyard's real, make contact with any officers there, assess what resources they have, and report back. We're going to need all the firepower we can get."

Jax straightened, determination hardening his gaze. "We'll find it."

Gathering his team in a briefing room, Jax detailed the mission. Rafe's eyes lit up at the mention of piloting a Shadow-class fighter.

"Finally!" Rafe grinned, the stealth fighter's reputation for agility and undetectability firing his excitement.

McHenry, on the other hand, crossed his arms and groaned. "A bomber? Seriously, Jax? You're sticking me with that flying brick?"

Jax smirked. "You're the best with heavy ordnance. And if we find this shipyard, we may need some extra muscle."

McHenry muttered something under his breath but made no further objections.

As the team moved toward their fighters, Cassian caught up to Bringi. After a tense moment, he spoke quietly. "Bringi... I'm sorry. I've been off lately, and you didn't deserve that."

Bringi looked up in surprise, her expression softening. "I don't know what's been going on, Cassian, but I'm glad you're finally saying something."

Cassian sighed, running a hand through his hair. "When we get back, I'll tell you everything. You deserve to know."

A small smile tugged at Bringi's lips. "Well, now you have to survive this mission, just so I can get those answers."

Cassian chuckled, some of the tension in his eyes easing. "Guess I do."

Soon after, Raptor Squadron launched from the *McIvey*, the void of space stretching before them as they closed in on the rumored shipyard's coordinates. The darkness of space seemed to stretch endlessly, a backdrop to the dangerous unknown lying ahead.

Approaching the coordinates, the system was hauntingly silent, stars glinting against the vast emptiness. Then, a large silhouette began to take shape, emerging from the darkness—a colossal structure, its imposing bulk gradually revealing itself.

"There it is," Cassian murmured over the comms, a mix of awe and apprehension in his voice. "It's real."

The Imperial shipyard loomed before them, a sprawling web of metal and machinery floating in the void. Docking platforms jutted out from the central hub, massive cranes and construction arms frozen mid-task, giving the place an abandoned, haunting appearance.

Scattered around the shipyard were half-constructed capital ships. Some gleamed with fresh armor plates, others were skeletal frames waiting for their outer layers. Destroyers, cruisers, and even a massive battleship frame towered above them, evidence of an Imperial arsenal in the making.

"Look at those ships," McHenry muttered, glancing out from his Mauler bomber. "They're building an entire fleet here."

"This could be exactly what we need—if it's still ours," Bringi said, her voice tinged with hope.

But Jax felt something was off. The shipyard was active, but there was no sign of crew. No shuttles moving between ships, no lights indicating work in progress. Switching to an open comm channel, Jax hailed the shipyard.

"This is Lieutenant Jax Ryland of the *McIvey*. We're on an Imperial mission. Requesting confirmation and response."

Only silence replied. Frowning, Jax tried again. "Shipyard command, respond. We are friendlies."

The moment stretched, then warning lights blared on Jax's instrument panel. Multiple signals filled the HUD.

"Contacts!" Rafe's voice crackled over the comms, urgent. "Hostiles, closing in fast!"

From the shipyard, a squadron of sleek, black fighters launched into space, their engines flaring as they accelerated toward Raptor Squadron. Sleek and streamlined, these ships lacked any visible cockpit, moving with an inhuman precision.

"They're not friendly!" Jax growled, his hands gripping the controls. "Form up! Weapons hot!"

Jax's Predator-class fighter banked hard as the enemy drones closed the distance. Their movements were disturbingly sharp, unnatural, with the precision of machines. He quickly locked onto one of the drones, firing off a quick burst from his blasters. The drone evaded with flawless timing, his shots barely grazing its hull.

"These are drones!" Rafe shouted. "No pilot signatures. They're controlled by the shipyard!"

Bringi veered sharply, narrowly avoiding a volley of laser fire from a trio of drones on her tail. "We're dealing with automated defenses—and they're designed to kill."

Cassian rolled his fighter into a tight turn, firing on a drone that had maneuvered in front of him. The drone twisted in mid-flight, avoiding his fire and countering with a precise burst of blaster fire that rocked Cassian's shields.

"These things are faster than anything we've fought before!" Cassian grunted, diving into a defensive spiral.

Jax watched the drones move in perfect, deadly formation, their firepower relentless. "We can't fight them like human pilots—there's no hesitation. They calculate every move."

But Raptor Squadron's advantage was their experience and adaptability. Rafe, flying his nimble Shadow-class fighter, darted through the drone formation, picking off one from below with a quick burst. McHenry's Mauler bomber brought the heavy firepower, scattering clusters of drones with each cannon blast. Bringi, her piloting as sharp as ever, weaved between the drones, using her fighter's agility to evade and fire with pinpoint accuracy.

Jax rolled out of a dive, looping behind two drones that were chasing McHenry. Firing on both, he watched one explode, its parts spiraling out in zero gravity, while the other tried to escape but was clipped by Bringi's blasters, sending it into a spin.

"Keep them split up!" Jax ordered. "They can't improvise like us. Use it against them."

Cassian looped around to flank two drones, his shots precise as he targeted the weak points, sending each drone into a burst of flame. "Nice call, Jax!"

The squadron began thinning the drone ranks, their tactics slowly overpowering the AI's programming. But the fight was far from over—more drones emerged from the shipyard, forming tighter, more aggressive attack patterns as they adapted.

"These things aren't going to stop," McHenry warned, taking out two drones with a powerful salvo. "We'll need to disable them at the source."

Jax scanned the shipyard, spotting an open hangar bay that looked like a maintenance hub. "There—if we get inside, we might find the control systems."

"Rafe, McHenry, cover us out here!" Jax ordered. "Cassian, Bringi, you're with me."

The three fighters dove toward the hangar bay, weaving through relentless streams of drone fire. Jax's heart pounded as he angled into the opening, the darkness of the hangar swallowing them whole. Behind them, Rafe and McHenry held the swarm at bay, blasting drones out of the void with every shot.

They had stepped into the heart of the storm, ready to face whatever the AI had waiting for them.

Chapter 33: Black Book Station

As Jax, Cassian, and Bringi stepped out of their fighters onto the hangar floor, they found themselves surrounded by Imperial soldiers, their weapons raised and expressions grim. A tense silence filled the air until a commanding voice rang out across the bay.

"Stand down," an officer in an Imperial Intelligence uniform ordered, his tone cold and unyielding, though with a hint of curiosity.

Jax, his helmet tucked under his arm, stepped forward, unphased. "Lieutenant Jax. We're here on an Imperial mission. And you are?"

The officer's expression remained steely, his gaze assessing. "My name is classified. What I want to know is why you've brought your people Black Book Station."

Jax studied him carefully, sensing this was someone unlikely to be swayed by pleasantries. "We didn't know it was your station," Jax said finally. "Our orders were to recon this location and see if it could support the fleet. The Empire's in crisis. Have you had any contact with the core?"

The officer's face remained impassive, but something in his posture shifted. "No," he replied. "This station has been on a communication lockdown per our protocols. A day ago, Imperial Navy ships attacked us without warning, no communications, just weapons fire. We defended ourselves but assumed you were a follow-up attack."

Jax shook his head. "We're not your enemy. The Navy's compromised—a rogue AI has taken over our ships. The Empire is on the brink. Gaia Prime is under siege, barely holding out with its planetary defenses."

For a long moment, the officer stood silent, weighing Jax's words. Finally, he nodded, his expression less guarded but no less wary. "Follow me."

Jax held up a hand, his tone firm. "Not until you call off your drones. We still have pilots out there."

The officer's gaze flicked to the hangar, his stance relaxing further as he keyed his comm and spoke a few clipped commands, then motioned for Jax, Bringi, and Cassian to follow him.

They moved through the station's dim corridors, industrial hallways lined with armored bulkheads and flickering lights. Though the tension remained palpable, the soldiers' postures softened, recognizing the shift in tone. Finally, the officer led them into a crew lounge off the hangar—sterile and functional, a table and a few metal chairs occupying the center.

The officer remained by the door, arms crossed, as Jax explained the dire situation the Empire was facing: the AI's hold over Imperial ships, the siege on Gaia Prime, and the fleet's rapid losses. As Jax spoke, the officer's expression grew darker.

"This station is a classified research and development facility," he said, voice clipped. "We've been studying technology recovered from the Vanguard War. That's all I can tell you."

Jax gave a grim nod. "We could use everything you've got. Ships, weapons, tech—whatever you can spare."

The officer's lips tightened, and he gave a brisk nod. "I'll confer with my command staff. In the meantime, your remaining pilots are cleared to land in the hangar, and quarters will be provided for all of you."

Jax relayed the message to Rafe and McHenry, and within moments, the Shadow-class fighter and Mauler bomber touched down in the hangar. Soon after, the squadron was escorted to temporary quarters—modest rooms but a welcome respite after the chaotic mission.

Cassian lingered in his quarters, turning over the conversation with the officer in his mind. But a different thought weighed even heavier on him. Something unresolved. With a determined breath, he stood and headed down the hall, stopping in front of Bringi's door. She opened it, eyes softening when she saw him standing there.

"Cassian?"

He hesitated, then stepped inside, letting the door close behind him. "We need to talk. I... owe you an explanation."

Bringi motioned for him to sit, but he remained standing, pacing slightly as he gathered his thoughts. "It's about what happened with... Vigil. The AI, the alternate you. I haven't been fair to you, and that's on me."

He recounted everything, from the alternate Bringi, her descent into darkness, and the emotional toll it had taken on him. Bringi listened in silence, her face unreadable at first, but her expression softened into understanding. She had questions—what it had been like, how much of it felt real—but Cassian answered as best as he could, though he, too, was left with questions.

"I didn't know what to think after that," Cassian admitted, his voice low. "It twisted my mind. I couldn't separate you from her... and that wasn't fair."

Bringi rose, stepping closer. "I understand, Cassian. You went through something I can barely imagine. But you have to know—I'm not her."

Cassian looked into her eyes, the weight of the past weeks lifting slightly. "I know. I'm sorry I pushed you away. I should have told you."

She offered a small, encouraging smile, her hand resting gently on his arm. "I'm just glad you finally did."

Then, without warning, Bringi leaned in, her lips brushing against his. Cassian's heart skipped a beat, but instinct took over, and he kissed her back, his hand reaching up to cradle her face. The connection he felt in that moment, something he hadn't let himself feel, brought him a sense of peace that he'd missed.

They pulled back for a brief moment, both a little breathless, and Bringi's eyes sparkled with a mischievous glint. "Promise me one thing," she murmured.

Cassian raised an eyebrow. "What's that?"

A playful smile tugged at her lips. "Swear you won't go psycho and start hunting down alternate versions of me."

Cassian chuckled, the tension dissolving. "I swear."

She laughed softly before pulling him into another kiss, this one deeper, more certain. Cassian's heart raced, but he allowed himself to let go, to simply be there in the moment with her. The room seemed to fade away, leaving only the two of them, grounding each other in the chaos surrounding them. The worries of the mission, the memories of the past few weeks, and the looming threat outside seemed to disappear, if only for a little while.

For now, they had each other, and that was enough.

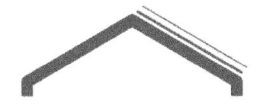

Chapter 34: Captain Barlow

The next morning, Jax and his team were escorted back to the hangar by the Black Book officer, who was as cryptic as ever. His expression remained unreadable as he addressed the squadron.

"We can provide a supply ship, loaded with food, water, weapons, and provisions," the officer announced in a measured tone. "It'll serve as a relief effort for your station, nothing more. Additionally, we can spare one gunship that should be resistant to the AI—though it'll only have a skeleton crew. It's not much, but it's all we can offer right now."

Jax gave a nod, knowing it was more than he'd expected. The officer continued, "If you encounter any ships or drones controlled by the rogue AI, try to disable them and bring them back here. Our team might be able to analyze the tech and develop a countermeasure."

With those parting words, Jax and his team departed Black Book Station, the supply ship and gunship in tow as they prepared to jump back to the refueling station. As they arrived, the station's beleaguered state became painfully clear—battle scars still marred the hull, and there was a lingering sense of tension among the crew. Jax coordinated the docking of the supply ship and gunship before heading to debrief Dalen.

Commander Dalen met Jax with a look of weary relief. "The supplies will help," Dalen admitted. "And the gunship is better than nothing, but where in the galaxy are we supposed to find enough crew to man it?"

Jax nodded, understanding his skepticism. "I get it. They're doing what they can, but... Black Book Station gives me an uneasy feeling. They've been in isolation too long, and their priorities feel... off."

Dalen sighed, his gaze growing distant. "I share your suspicions. Next time we go back, I'll join you. We need to know what's really going on there." He paused, then added, "But for now, we'll use what they've given us. It's all we've got."

Before they could continue, the station's alarms blared, cutting through the conversation. Dalen's comm crackled as a station officer's voice came through, tense and urgent: "Commander, an unknown ship just jumped into the system. They're launching fighters—unknown design."

Jax was already sprinting toward the hangar, signaling his team. "Scramble! We're heading up."

Within moments, Jax, Cassian, Bringi, and the rest of Raptor Squadron were back in their cockpits. Rafe took his Shadow-class recon fighter, while McHenry grumbled, strapping into his Mauler bomber again. The others manned their Predator-class fighters. They launched from the station, weapons primed, ready to engage.

Jax scanned the battlefield through his HUD. The system registered a Wraith gunship, flanked by a formation of sleek, unfamiliar fighters. Yet, oddly, the Wraith forces hadn't opened fire; they maintained a defensive formation, holding position near the edge of the station's perimeter.

"Hold your fire," Jax ordered over the comms, his voice steady but cautious. "Something's off."

Keying in a comms link, Jax hailed the gunship. There was a tense pause before a gravelly, weathered voice responded.

"This is Captain Barlow of the Wraiths," the voice growled. "We've come to talk."

Jax's heart raced with a mix of skepticism and shock. The Wraiths had never approached peacefully before. Shaking off his disbelief, he responded, "Barlow, hold your position. I need to get my orders."

Switching to Dalen's frequency, Jax spoke quickly. "Commander, you heard that?"

Dalen's voice came through, laced with both surprise and exhaustion. "I heard it. This is… unexpected."

Jax could sense Dalen carefully considering the options. "Escort them aboard the station," Dalen finally ordered. "We'll have marines waiting in the hangar bay. At this point, we can't afford to pass up a chance to find out what they're after."

Jax acknowledged the command and switched back to the Wraith frequency. "Captain Barlow, you're clear to approach the station. But be advised, marines will be waiting. This had better be a peaceful talk."

Barlow's voice came back, rough but calm. "We're not here to fight. We'll honor that, as long as your men do the same."

Jax led the way, escorting the Wraith gunship and its mysterious fighters toward the station. The tension among Raptor Squadron was palpable. Bringi's voice came through Jax's private channel.

"Do you think they're telling the truth?" she asked, her voice low.

Jax was silent for a moment, running through the possibilities in his mind. The Wraiths had been their enemies for as long as he could remember—it was hard to believe they would ever stand down, let alone approach for a talk. But something about this felt different, a kind of desperation.

"I guess we'll find out," he replied.

Chapter 35: Unlikely Allies

The hangar bay buzzed with tension as Captain Barlow's heavily armed shuttle touched down with a metallic thud. The marines stationed around the landing area stood alert, weapons ready, their armor gleaming under the hangar's dim lighting. Jax and his squadron had already disembarked their fighters and now observed from the edge of the bay, each wary. Bringi exchanged a brief, meaningful glance with Cassian, both on guard.

The shuttle's ramp hissed open, releasing a puff of steam. Emerging from the shadows was Captain Barlow, whose very presence commanded attention. Tall and muscular, he had the hardened look of a man shaped by endless battles and the unforgiving depths of space. His pale skin contrasted sharply with the thick, dark beard spilling untamed across his face, and a black patch covered one eye, giving him a distinctly piratical air. A long, worn cloak billowed as he moved, and strapped to his side were a cutlass and a well-worn pistol. Every step seemed calculated, yet devoid of malice—only a quiet, almost resigned authority.

"I came alone," Barlow said, his voice gravelly yet calm. He raised his hands slightly, a gesture of peace, as he eyed the six fully armed marines standing between him and the crew lounge. "A sign of good faith."

The marines, led by Sergeant Varek, didn't lower their guard, but they nodded and moved into escort formation, guiding Barlow through the hangar's bulkhead and into the crew lounge. Inside, Commander Dalen, Jax, and Sergeant Varek waited in the dimly lit room, the air thick with expectation.

Dalen, ever the professional, extended his hand first. "Welcome aboard, Captain Barlow. Forgive my skepticism, but I have to wonder why the leader of the Wraiths would want to talk now."

Barlow's lips curled into a crooked grin. He shook Dalen's hand with a firm grip. "Fair enough, Commander. Pirates do love their secrets."

Jax, arms crossed and standing just behind Dalen, chimed in. "Imperial Intelligence has been trying for years to unmask the real leader of the Wraiths. And now here you are, alone and ready to talk. What's changed?"

Barlow sighed, letting his gaze wander the room, his one good eye assessing each of them in turn. "What's changed, Commander, is that I thought I had a good deal. When the Vanguard approached a while back, it looked like an opportunity—a way for the Wraiths to be more than a band of pirates. But halfway through the Vanguard-Empire war, something shifted. The Vanguard stopped being allies and took control of my entire operation." He clenched his fists, his frustration evident. "After those rangers, Butler and Antrim, took down the Vanguard, I started to rebuild."

Dalen and Jax exchanged a look, startled by the revelation.

"But then," Barlow continued, "ships started vanishing. At first, I thought it was remnants of the Empire or rogue factions picking us off. Then, our lost ships started coming back—only this time, they were under someone else's command."

Jax narrowed his eyes. "Someone else? You mean the rogue AI, don't you?"

Barlow nodded gravely. "My people found out it's called Nexus. I don't know how it happened or where it came from, but I'm certain Nexus is controlling those ships. My Wraiths have become pawns in this AI's game, and I'm done with it. I'm not about to be anyone's puppet, least of all a machine playing God."

Jax, still skeptical, pressed further. "Why not retreat to one of your hideouts? I can't imagine you or what's left of your organization would care if the Empire burns."

Barlow gave a hearty laugh. "You're wrong! We're pirates, not anarchists. What's the point of being a pirate if there's nothing left to plunder?"

"So, once this is over, you go back to killing our people and robbing our ships?" Jax asked, arms crossed.

Barlow met his gaze steadily. "Once this is over, I doubt things will ever go back to the way they were for any of us."

Jax frowned, realizing Barlow was likely right.

Dalen crossed his arms, observing Barlow intently. The pirate's frustration was evident, but there was a sincerity in his words neither he nor Jax could ignore.

"So, what do you want from us?" Dalen asked cautiously.

Barlow's voice hardened. "I want to offer my services. The Wraiths may be pirates, but we're damn good at what we do. I have ships, and I have people—those still loyal to me. I'm tired of fighting Nexus alone. We join forces, and together, we can bring down this AI. I'm not asking for amnesty or forgiveness. I just want a fair fight."

Dalen raised an eyebrow, weighing the offer. Jax shot him a look, one that spoke volumes—they were low on resources, allies, and time. If Barlow was sincere, this could be the advantage they needed.

"Give us a moment," Dalen said, motioning for Jax to step aside with him. In a quiet corner, they lowered their voices.

"What do you think?" Dalen asked.

Jax frowned but nodded. "We can't afford to turn down help, not now. Nexus is too big a threat, and if the Wraiths are under its control, we'll need every ally we can get. Barlow's angry, but I believe him."

Dalen rubbed his temples, deep in thought. "I don't trust him entirely, but I don't think we have much choice. The rogue AI is a greater danger than we anticipated."

After a moment's consideration, Dalen turned back to Barlow, extending his hand again.

"We'll take your help," Dalen said. "But know this, Captain Barlow—if you cross us, there won't be anywhere in this galaxy for you to hide."

Barlow chuckled darkly, gripping Dalen's hand firmly. "I'd expect nothing less, Commander. We have a lot to discuss."

"Indeed we do," Dalen replied in a somber tone.

As the tension in the room began to ease, Jax felt a surge of resolve. They had found an unlikely ally in Captain Barlow and his Wraiths, but the threat of Nexus loomed larger than ever. The fight was far from over.

Chapter 36: Wraiths And Imperials

Over the next few days, the refueling station—now christened "Ally Station"—became a bustling hive of activity. Wraith ships, from frigates to corvettes, and even a few larger vessels, jumped into the system, nearly doubling the size of Dalen's fleet. What was once a quiet outpost now thrummed with the sounds of repair crews, supply drops, and the heavy hum of engines coming online.

Captain Barlow had kept his word, providing enough crew to man the gunship gifted by Black Book Station. However, integrating the pirate crews into the disciplined ranks of the Imperial Navy was no small task.

In one of the ship's training rooms, Imperial naval officers barked orders at the ragtag Wraith recruits. The pirates, long accustomed to the unrestrained and chaotic life aboard Wraith ships, chafed under the strict regimen of naval procedures. Lieutenant Hale, visibly frustrated, watched as a group of Wraiths stumbled through basic formation drills.

"This isn't a bar fight, lads!" Hale shouted, pacing back and forth. "When I tell you to form up, you form up. When I tell you to man a station, you don't wander off to check your weapons. This is a navy vessel!"

One pirate with a missing tooth and tattoos covering his arms leaned against a console, clearly bored. "Aye, but on our ships, we don't got all these 'rules.' We do what works."

"What works," Hale snapped, "is getting your shipmates killed if you don't follow orders. Discipline is the only thing that's going to keep this ship intact under fire."

The pirate spat on the floor, earning a sharp glare from Hale, but the officer kept his composure. It was clear this would be an uphill battle. These Wraiths were skilled fighters, but they had little concept of the rigid structure needed to keep a navy ship functioning in combat. Still, they had no choice but to learn.

Nearby, Captain Barlow watched with a bemused expression as another group of pirates fumbled with the ship's advanced systems. Two of them struggled with targeting sensors, accidentally triggering a diagnostic mode that set off a cascade of alarms. The overseeing naval officer threw up his hands in exasperation.

"Pirates and discipline," Barlow muttered to himself, shaking his head. "This should be interesting."

A few days later, Barlow summoned Dalen and Jax to the briefing room on Ally Station. The flickering holo-map of Wraith space cast a blue glow over the walls as Barlow stood with his hands clasped behind his back, his imposing figure silhouetted against the stars.

"I've got a mission for you," Barlow said without preamble.

Jax, seated beside Dalen, raised an eyebrow. "What kind of mission?"

Barlow tapped a button on the holo-map, zooming in on a remote, desolate planet deep within Wraith territory. "Several of my ships are grounded here, hidden from Nexus forces. But there's a problem—a small Nexus capital ship is in orbit, being used as a communications hub. If my ships try to break atmosphere, that Nexus vessel will rip them apart before they can power up their shields."

Dalen examined the map, his brow furrowed. "And you want us to deal with the Nexus ship."

Barlow nodded. "Your fighters are small and fast. You could engage the Nexus ship, keeping it occupied long enough for my grounded ships to get airborne and power up their defenses. Once they're in the air, we'll have a fighting chance to take down that capital ship."

Jax crossed his arms, his expression skeptical. "And once those Wraith ships are in the air, will they help us fight the Nexus forces or vanish back into the black?"

Barlow's eye gleamed. "You have my word, Ranger. These ships will fight alongside you. We're all in this together now."

Dalen exchanged a look with Jax. "But there's a catch, isn't there?"

Barlow grinned. "One of my men will go with you—a pilot who'll vouch for your squadron when you reach the planet. The Wraiths down there are skittish and won't trust Imperials on sight, but they'll listen to one of their own."

Jax immediately shook his head. "Absolutely not. I'm not taking one of your pirates into a battle with my squadron. That's a liability I can't afford."

Barlow's grin faded, his tone sharpening. "If you want my ships in the fight, you'll need my man. The Wraiths on the ground won't launch without him—they won't know who to trust."

The two men locked eyes, tension crackling between them. Finally, Dalen stepped in. "Jax, we need this. If Barlow's man can get those ships in the air, we'll have the firepower we need."

Jax clenched his jaw but finally nodded. "Fine. But he follows my orders."

Barlow smirked. "You'll like him. His name's Purdue."

As the fighters launched from Ally Station, Jax couldn't shake his unease. Purdue, flying in his Wraith fighter behind the squadron, had been tight-lipped throughout the pre-flight briefing. When Jax had pressed him on his experience, Purdue had shrugged and muttered something vague about having "flown a few missions."

The Nexus capital ship loomed as they approached the planet's atmosphere, a sleek, foreboding vessel bristling with turrets and sensors. As soon as it detected Jax's squadron, its fighters scrambled to intercept.

"Here we go," Jax muttered. "Stay tight. We need to keep them busy long enough for the Wraith ships to launch."

Rafe, in his Shadow-class recon fighter, banked left, drawing the first wave of Nexus drones away from the planet. McHenry, piloting his Mauler, took a more direct approach, skimming low over the Nexus ship's hull and unleashing a volley of fire to draw its attention.

"Raptor Squadron, break formation and engage!" Jax ordered, diving into a swarm of Nexus drones. His ship shuddered as laser fire scraped his shields, but he held his course, weaving through the chaos to break up the enemy formations.

Meanwhile, down on the planet's surface, Barlow's grounded ships sprang to life. Engines roared as they powered up, and one by one, the Wraith frigates began their ascent, thrusters flaring as they broke through the clouds.

The Nexus ship wasn't about to let them escape. It shifted its focus to the ascending Wraith ships, turrets blazing.

"McHenry, cover the Wraiths! Keep that thing off them!" Jax shouted.

McHenry swung his Mauler into the fray, unleashing heavy ordnance at the Nexus ship's gun emplacements. Rafe continued harassing the Nexus fighters, expertly keeping them scattered and off-balance.

Suddenly, Purdue's voice crackled over the comm. "Wraith ships are clear. Get ready for them to join the fun."

Moments later, the Wraith ships opened fire, sending a barrage of plasma bolts tearing into the Nexus ship's shields. With the combined firepower of Raptor Squadron and the Wraiths, the Nexus vessel's defenses began to buckle.

"Let's finish this!" Jax roared, leading the squadron in a final attack run.

The Nexus ship buckled under the relentless assault. Its shields flickered and failed, leaving its hull vulnerable to the pounding onslaught. Explosions rippled across its surface as internal systems ruptured, fires blazing through its structure. A final volley from McHenry's Mauler struck the ship's power core, triggering a chain reaction that tore through the Nexus vessel. It disintegrated in a blinding burst of fire and twisted metal, debris scattering into the void.

The Wraith ships were free, and the immediate threat was neutralized—for now.

As they regrouped in orbit, Jax exhaled a breath he hadn't realized he was holding. Purdue's voice came over the comms again, a hint of approval in his tone. "Not bad for a bunch of Imperials."

Jax rolled his eyes but allowed himself a faint smile. Despite everything, they'd made it through—just one victory in a war that was far from over.

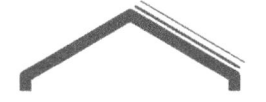

Chapter 37: Good News, Bad News

The mood in the briefing room was tense but focused. Senior officers from both the Imperial Navy and the Wraiths sat around the circular table, with Captain Dalen at the head and Jax standing nearby. The room was dimly lit, and the flickering glow of the star map cast long shadows across the gathered faces. Imperials and pirates sitting side by side was a strange sight, but desperate times had forged strange alliances.

Raptor Squadron and Purdue had returned from their mission to free the Wraith ships, with the newly liberated vessels swelling the ranks of what was now formally designated the Rescue Fleet. This ragtag fleet of Imperial warships and Wraith frigates floated around Ally Station, their purpose clear: to counter Nexus's tightening grip on the Steele Empire.

Jax, his flight suit still streaked with grime from hours in the cockpit, took a seat beside Captain Dalen as the meeting began.

Dalen stood, gesturing to the holographic map hovering above the table. The image shifted to focus on Gaia Prime, the Empire's home world, now surrounded by a glowing outline representing a Nexus blockade.

"Our scouts have been jumping in and out of the Gaia system, monitoring the siege of Gaia Prime," Dalen began, his voice steady but heavy. "Nexus forces have stopped direct assaults on the planetary shield. Instead, they've formed a blockade, and it appears they've brought in the majority of their fleet."

There were murmurs around the table. The blockade was a dire concern, though the silver lining was evident.

"The planetary shield is still holding strong," Dalen continued. "Gaia Prime has enough reserves of food, water, and energy to endure for an extended period. But breaking the blockade is beyond our current capabilities."

Sergeant Varek, arms crossed as he leaned against the wall, grunted. "Good news for Gaia Prime, but we've got troops stranded across the Empire. Several marine units are stuck planetside on various colonies, holding off Nexus forces wherever they can. If we don't get them out soon, they'll be overrun."

Dalen nodded. "Get me their positions and numbers, Sergeant. We'll extract and redeploy them to protect key civilian populations. Nexus won't ignore the colonies forever."

Varek gave a sharp nod, already preparing the details.

Next, Lieutenant Commander Rosali, head of operations at Ally Station, spoke up. "With the influx of Wraith personnel, we've managed to get nearly every combat-worthy vessel online. As for fuel, munitions, and supplies, we're stocked to operate for another five months if we stay efficient."

It was a welcome bit of good news, but the shadow of Nexus loomed over them all.

Dalen then turned to Captain Barlow. "Captain, anything to report on your end?"

Barlow leaned back, stroking his beard before answering. "I've had scouts checking a few of your Imperial systems. We found something interesting at Griffin IV." He tapped a button, and the map zoomed in on a planet far from Gaia Prime.

"Griffin IV?" Rosali searched her datapad. "That's one of our largest munitions plants."

Jax raised an eyebrow. "Why does that matter? We're stocked for now."

Barlow's voice was low, laced with tension. "It's only guarded by two Nexus drone carriers. Those carriers control all the drones in that system. And I believe you wanted deactivated drones for study?" He glanced at Dalen.

Dalen blinked in surprise. "We could use those drones, but... what's your angle, Barlow?"

Barlow smirked. "I get to hurt Nexus, for one. And while we have enough munitions now, a prolonged conflict could stretch us thin. Capturing Griffin IV would mean a renewable source of weapons."

Dalen scratched his chin thoughtfully. "Right now, what we have is all we have. Securing the plant could be a game-changer."

Rosali, without looking up from her datapad, added, "The Griffin system also has several mining complexes and ore refineries. Mostly to support the munitions plant, but if we get to the point of building ships again, it could be invaluable."

Dalen nodded. "But this means taking the system—and occupying it. We'll have to neutralize those drone carriers."

Jax's eyes lit up as an idea formed. "If we disable even one of the carriers, the drones it deployed would go dormant. We could capture them intact and undamaged. That would give us a wealth of Nexus tech to study and reverse engineer."

Dalen considered this. "It sounds promising. But how do we capture a drone carrier without destroying it?"

Jax began pacing as he formulated a plan. "There's an old Imperial missile boat in the Rescue Fleet—I saw it docked earlier."

Barlow nodded. "That one's mine. She's still got teeth."

"If we strip the missile pods and replace them with ion cannons, we could overload the carrier's shields," Jax suggested. "Then we load our Maulers with ion pulse torpedoes and disable the carrier's systems just long enough to capture it."

Rosali's eyes lit up with interest. "And once the carrier is down?"

Dalen picked up the thread. "We bring in a tug from just outside the system to tow the carrier and its drones to Black Book Station for analysis."

Barlow's eyes narrowed. "Black Book Station? And what exactly is that?"

The room went silent, and Dalen stiffened, his voice dropping. "That's classified."

Barlow stood, his posture challenging. "You want my ships, my men, and my support, and you're keeping secrets? What else are you not telling me?"

Tension thickened in the room as Dalen and Barlow locked eyes, the air practically crackling with confrontation.

Jax stepped between them, raising his hands. "Enough! We're not risking this alliance over classified intel. Barlow, the Wraiths haven't laid all their cards on the table, either. We need mutual trust to pull this off. We're in this fight together, and we don't have the luxury of wasting time."

Barlow's jaw tightened, but he stepped back, his voice grudging. "Fine. But remember this, Dalen: we're partners now. I expect transparency."

Dalen's nod was curt, his face tense but resolute. "Understood. We'll brief you on what's relevant."

The two men shook hands again, their truce fragile but intact.

Dalen turned to the officers around the table. "Prepare your ships and crews. We hit Griffin IV in 48 hours. Jax, get that missile boat retrofitted and your fighters ready. We're taking those carriers and those drones."

Jax saluted, his mind already racing with logistics. It was a risky mission, but the potential payoff was too great to ignore.

As the officers filed out, Jax lingered, watching Dalen and Barlow exchange a few more terse words. The alliance was fragile, but it would hold—for now. With Griffin IV on the horizon, the Rescue Fleet had its next objective.

Chapter 38: Mission To Griffin IV

The Rescue Fleet's assault group floated in the cold silence of space, ready to jump into the Griffin IV system. The formation was a balanced mix of fighters, bombers, and the heavily modified Imperial missile boat, all poised for what could be a pivotal strike. Jax sat in the cockpit of his Predator-class fighter, eyes scanning the assembled fleet, his focus unwavering. Every ship was vital, and every detail counted on this mission.

"All systems green," reported Bringi, her voice calm but betraying the tension simmering beneath the surface. Jax knew this mission had to succeed.

He keyed open the comm to the strike force. "Listen up, everyone. Raptor Squadron is going after the first drone carrier. The rest of you are escorting the missile boat and Maulers to hit the second. Stick to the plan, and keep those drones off our backs long enough for the ion weapons to do their job. We'll disable that second carrier and get out of here."

The fleet awaited his final command.

"Jump!" Jax ordered.

The stars stretched into streaks as the fleet blinked into hyperspace.

The Rescue Fleet's strike group emerged in perfect formation in the Griffin IV system. Below them, the lush green-and-blue planet glimmered, but their target lay above it: two Nexus drone carriers, each a hulking fortress surrounded by swarms of drones.

"Drone formations incoming!" Bringi warned over the comms as the Nexus drones detached from the carriers, hurtling towards the fleet.

"Raptor Squadron, with me!" Jax commanded, throwing his fighter into a hard turn toward the first carrier. His squadron followed, twelve sleek Predator-class starfighters diving into the mass of drones.

Jax weaved through the chaos, his reflexes sharp as he dodged blasts of fire from the drones. His targeting system locked onto one of the carrier's drone control towers, a critical structure jutting from the smooth hull. "Engage!"

The Predator-Class fighters unleashed a barrage of missiles, streaking toward the carrier. Explosions rippled across its surface, but the drones continued their assault with relentless precision. A drone veered dangerously close to Jax's wing, forcing him into a hard juke. "Stay tight! Don't get separated!"

A fresh swarm of drones poured from the carrier's interior, swarming Raptor Squadron with deadly intent. Jax maneuvered furiously, dodging both laser blasts and drones attempting kamikaze runs against his fighter.

A quick glance at his tactical readout showed his squad mates also on the verge of being overwhelmed. Just then, several Wraith fighters broke off from their own engagement and swooped in to support Raptor Squadron.

One Wraith launched a missile that struck a drone in the midst of a dense cluster. The resulting explosion, amplified by the drone's power core, set off a chain reaction, clearing out a large section of the swarm. The drones quickly adapted, spreading out, which made them easier targets for Raptor Squadron.

"We're being targeted by the carrier!" Cassian shouted as exhaust trails streaked from the Nexus ship toward them.

"Go evasive, make attack runs when you can," Jax ordered, leading his fighter into a pass along the carrier's hull, his squadron in tow.

Missiles detonated around them, drone wreckage spinning off into the void as Raptor Squadron pressed their attack. Jax watched as the carrier's hull began to fracture under the pounding assault.

"Target the core!" Jax commanded, lining up a perfect shot. The squadron's firepower converged on the drone carrier's core, triggering a brilliant explosion as the carrier finally shattered.

The first drone carrier was down.

Across the battlefield, the missile boat and the Maulers were engaged in their own high-stakes dance. Once an Imperial relic, the missile boat now sported powerful, modified ion cannons intended to overload the second carrier's shields. The Maulers, equipped with ion pulse torpedoes, circled, ready to disable rather than destroy.

"Missile boat, you're up! Overload those shields!" a Predator pilot called, leading the escort.

The missile boat surged forward, weaving through incoming drone fire. Ion beams arced from its cannons, slamming into the Nexus carrier's shields, ripples of distortion spreading across the barrier.

"Shields holding—keep firing!" the pilot urged.

The ion cannons roared again, concentrated bursts pounding the shield until it flickered, struggling to withstand the assault.

"Hurry it up!" the missile boat pilot shouted, strain clear in his voice. "Our power relays won't take much more."

Just then, the carrier's shield flickered and collapsed.

"Now! Maulers, launch!" The Maulers swooped in, their bomb bays opening as ion pulse torpedoes streaked toward the exposed carrier. The drones scrambled to intercept, but fighter squadrons engaged them, buying precious seconds.

The torpedoes found their mark, releasing a surge of electrical energy that pulsed through the carrier, shorting out its systems. One by one, the drones around it went dark, lifeless as they fell toward the planet below. The carrier's lights sputtered, then went out entirely.

As calm settled over the battlefield, Jax's voice crackled over the comms. "Drones are inactive. Begin recovery. Shuttles, move in."

Shuttles began winking into the system from nearby, their cargo bays open to retrieve the dormant Nexus drones, placing each one carefully into holding cells within the disabled carrier.

"The tug's inbound," Jax reported. Right on cue, the tug vessel blinked into existence, homing in on the carrier.

Jax opened a channel to the planet below. "This is Raptor Squadron, Rescue Fleet. Do you copy, munitions plant?"

Static crackled before a voice came through. "We copy, Raptor Squadron. Situation here is stable. We have surplus munitions and can start transferring them to Ally Station if you establish the supply lines."

"We'll set them up," Jax replied, satisfied. "Stand by for further instructions."

Everything seemed to have gone according to plan—almost too smoothly. Jax felt a gnawing unease creeping in. The drones hadn't fought as fiercely as he'd expected, and Nexus hadn't deployed any significant countermeasures.

His suspicions were confirmed sooner than he'd hoped.

Before the tug could finish securing the carrier, an Imperial carrier blinked into the system at the far edge. Jax's scanner identified it immediately: SSV McIvey.

A second later, Dalen's voice came over the fleetwide comm. "Jax, I'm joining you on the trip to Black Book Station."

Jax clenched his jaw, a tight feeling settling in his gut. The McIvey's sudden arrival didn't sit right with him.

He opened a private comm to his wingmen, his tone cautious. "Stay sharp, people. I've got a feeling this isn't over yet."

Chapter 39: Taking Black Book Station

The SSV *McIvey*, Raptor Squadron, and the tug carrying the disabled Nexus drone carrier entered the shadowy expanse around Black Book Station. The station loomed ahead, hidden deep within the void, an imposing silhouette that held untold secrets. Jax felt the weight of those secrets, like a heavy anchor pulling him down.

Dalen's shuttle docked in the station's hangar, and the tug, following orders from Black Book Station, disengaged from the Nexus carrier. Dalen, Jax, Sergeant Varek, and two Imperial Marines stepped off the shuttle, their footsteps echoing across the cold metal floor. Waiting for them was the same unnamed intelligence officer Jax had encountered during his last visit.

"Thank you for delivering this valuable prize," the officer said smoothly, his face unreadable. "We'll take it from here. Have the tug disengage and leave the system immediately."

Dalen's voice was firm, commanding. "I'm the ranking Imperial naval officer in this sector, and I'm here to conduct an inspection. This is a matter of Empire-wide security."

The officer's polite demeanor didn't falter. "Black Book Station operates under the direct supervision of the Director of Imperial Intelligence, independent of any other Imperial command. You have no authority here, Commander Dalen."

Dalen bristled, his voice rising. "These aren't normal circumstances. The Empire is under siege, and we're all that stands between it and collapse. If you refuse, I'll bring in every ship in the Rescue Fleet and a full platoon of marines to secure this station."

"Once again, Commander," the officer replied, maddeningly calm, "you have no authority here. Imperial Intelligence operates outside the military command structure."

"Except in exigent circumstances," Dalen shot back. "I'd say our current situation qualifies. You will comply, or we will take control of this entire station."

The intelligence officer's eyes narrowed, though his calm never wavered. "That would be a mistake, Commander, and it would not end well for you or your forces."

Unwilling to back down, Dalen gave the order. "Marines, take him into custody."

The marines moved swiftly, cuffing the officer's hands behind his back. But as they attempted to move past the hangar, they found the doors to the deeper levels of the station sealed.

Jax crossed his arms. "Locked out. Typical."

Sergeant Varek glanced at Dalen. "We can breach the door with explosives, sir."

Jax raised a hand. "Not yet." He activated his comms. "Rafe, I need you to land on the station. We've got some doors that need opening."

A few minutes later, Rafe's fighter touched down in the hangar, and he quickly began working on the door controls. Sensing this could escalate, Dalen called the *McIvey* to shuttle in additional marines.

The intelligence officer, still restrained, spoke up. "Commander, this is your last chance to leave before things get... worse. You have no clearance to know of our existence, let alone issue directives here."

Dalen ignored him. "Keep working, Rafe."

Without warning, the intelligence officer shouted, "Gamma Blackout Order 863!"

The command echoed through the hangar, and immediately alarms blared. The heavy hangar doors slammed shut, cutting off the route for the reinforcements about to land. At the same time, the sealed door leading deeper into the station slid open.

From the shadows beyond, a squad of robotic soldiers emerged. These weren't the hulking Nexus drones or the humanoid Vanguards—they were sleek, efficient, wearing the insignia of Imperial Intelligence. Their design was distinct, menacing, and they moved with precision, weapons trained on Jax, Dalen, Varek, Rafe, and the marines.

Despite his restraints, the intelligence officer smirked at Dalen. "You've just made your final mistake, Commander. Black Book Station is no place for outsiders. Now you'll learn what it means to challenge Imperial Intelligence."

Dalen's hand instinctively went to the blaster at his side. "You think a few drones are going to stop us?"

"These are merely the closest units," the officer replied smoothly. "There are more where they came from. Along with other... defenses."

Though Jax maintained his composure, he felt the tension mounting. "Stand down," he said quietly to the marines, not wanting to provoke a firefight. The marines glanced at Varek, who gave a reluctant nod, and they slowly complied.

Rafe looked over at Jax, datapad in hand. "I might be able to hack into their system, but it'll take time."

"We don't have time," Varek growled, one hand resting on his blaster. "One wrong move, and they'll open fire."

Dalen held his ground, his gaze fixed on the robotic soldiers, then shifted to the officer. "You still think you have the upper hand here, don't you?"

The officer's smug expression remained. "The Director is already aware of your actions, Commander. This station isn't merely a storage site for drones. If you push us, we'll respond with everything at our disposal."

Jax's mind raced. He couldn't shake the feeling that there was something far more sinister going on. Black Book Station, with all its secrecy, clearly held more than just drones.

"Jax," Rafe whispered, "if I can get into their systems, I might be able to disable the robots—or at least grant us access to the deeper levels. But we're surrounded, and it'll take a while."

Jax nodded, eyes narrowing as he surveyed the room. "Do it, but be careful. We're not just here for control. We need to understand what's really happening here."

Rafe got to work, his focus intense as he tapped into the station's systems. The marines kept their weapons lowered, but the atmosphere was taut, like a live wire ready to snap. The intelligence officer stood motionless, a look of satisfaction on his face as his robotic soldiers maintained their intimidating stance.

Jax leaned in, speaking low enough that only Dalen could hear. "This place is hiding something more than drones. We need to find out what it is before this escalates further."

Dalen's jaw tightened. "Agreed. But if this officer wants a fight, he's going to get one."

The intelligence officer's smile grew. "You have no idea what you've just stepped into, Commander."

As Rafe continued his hack, the alarms blared relentlessly—a reminder that time was running out.

Chapter 40: Pirates Will Pillage

In the cold darkness outside Black Book Station, Cassian listened intently to the comms chatter. His HUD flashed a warning as the marine shuttle pilot's voice crackled over the channel.

"The hangar doors have sealed. We're locked out from the inside!"

Cassian's eyes narrowed as he turned his fighter toward the station. "Raptor Squadron, form up on me," he ordered over the squadron's encrypted channel.

As the squadron raced toward the hangar, Cassian noticed something unsettling: armored panels had slid into place, sealing every viewport on the station. The sleek, black plating gave Black Book Station an eerie, impenetrable appearance.

Before he could react further, a cold, automated voice echoed over all Imperial frequencies. "All Imperial forces, vacate the system immediately. Black Book Station is under secure lockdown."

Cassian keyed his comm and responded firmly, "This is Lieutenant Cassian Gray of Raptor Squadron. What's the status of Commander Dalen and his team? They landed earlier."

The same emotionless voice replied, "They are now in our custody."

The channel went dead, leaving an ominous silence in the cockpit. Cassian cursed under his breath and opened a channel to the *McIvey*. "McIvey, call in reinforcements. We'll need backup from Ally Station and the Rescue Fleet. Commander Dalen and his team have been detained."

Just as Cassian prepared for what was likely to escalate into a full-blown confrontation, he caught sight of *The Sparrow*, Captain Barlow's flagship, exiting hyperspace nearby. Several Wraith ships followed, their ominous shapes casting long shadows. Shortly after, more Imperial Navy ships arrived, each a glimmer of hope—and a reminder of the risks if the Wraiths gained access to Black Book's prototype tech.

A blinking light on Cassian's console indicated an incoming transmission from *The Sparrow*.

Cassian opened the channel, and Barlow's voice filled his cockpit. "Cassian, hope you don't mind us dropping by. Thought you lads might be running into a spot of trouble."

Cassian couldn't help but grin. "And it had nothing to do with your curiosity about this station?"

Barlow chuckled. "Maybe a touch of that too. Anyway, we're here now. How can we help?"

Cassian took a moment before responding. "Captain, we're locked out, and Commander Dalen and his team are being held inside. I'm not sure what's happening in there, but I need your help to get our people out."

Barlow's voice held a hint of mischief. "Give me a few minutes, Lieutenant. I need to confer with my people."

As Barlow closed the channel, Cassian's fingers tightened around the control stick. Time was slipping away.

Inside Black Book Station's dimly lit hangar, tensions were reaching a boiling point. The intelligence officer, his smug demeanor unbroken, nodded to one of his robotic soldiers, who removed his restraints. With a glance, he spotted Rafe, crouched over a terminal, desperately trying to access the station's systems.

"Put them all in restraints," the officer commanded the robotic soldiers.

One of the Imperial Marines, refusing to surrender without a fight, lunged forward and managed to disable one of the robotic soldiers with a precise shot to its head. But before he could react further, another robot fired, and the marine collapsed, lifeless, onto the cold floor.

Sergeant Varek roared in fury, fists clenched, his entire body trembling. Jax and Rafe had to restrain him as the robotic soldiers cuffed the rest of the team and marched them through the station's labyrinthine corridors to a high-security brig deep in the heart of Black Book Station.

In the cold, dim cell, Jax leaned toward Rafe. "How far did you get before they caught you?"

Rafe shook his head in frustration. "Not far. Their encryption is top-tier. But I did see something strange. There are several labs and what looks like a ship manufacturing facility near the station's core."

Jax raised an eyebrow. "Why would they need shipbuilding inside the station? This place is more than just a research station. Who knows what kind of advanced tech they're hiding?"

In his office, the intelligence officer sat behind his desk, activating a secure holocomm channel. A holographic image flickered to life: Colonel Mitel, a stern-faced man with sharp eyes in an Imperial Intelligence uniform.

The officer swallowed as Mitel's gaze locked onto him. "Sir, we have a situation. Commander Dalen and a party of marines forced their way onto the station. I had no choice but to take them into custody."

Mitel's expression darkened. "Dalen and Jax are dangerous men. You should not have underestimated them."

The officer's voice wavered. "They forced my hand, sir. I—"

"Enough!" Mitel's tone was ice-cold. "Under no circumstances are you to harm any of the Imperial personnel in your custody. Do not initiate hostile actions against the ships outside. You've already made this situation worse than it needed to be."

The officer's face paled. "One marine has already been killed... by one of the robotic soldiers."

Mitel's hologram seemed to grow even colder. "You will take no further action until I arrive. I am coming personally to handle this."

Outside the station, Cassian received a response from Barlow.

"Cassian," Barlow began, his voice calm but sharp, "we have a plan to board the station, but my people... well, they're pirates by nature. If we go in, they'll pillage along the way."

Cassian's mind raced. Wraiths with access to Black Book Station's tech would be disastrous for the Empire. "Captain," he replied carefully, "if you could adjust that plan to get our marines onto the station, we might be able to avoid any... complications."

Barlow chuckled knowingly. "Figured you'd say that. Don't worry—I planned for it. We'll get your marines in. Just be ready. Once we breach, it'll be fast."

Cassian felt a flicker of hope mixed with a sense of dread. The situation was spiraling out of control, and the stakes had never been higher. If they couldn't regain control of Black Book Station, there was no telling what would happen next.

Back in the brig, Jax stared up at the ceiling, his mind racing. "Labs, ship manufacturing... what in the galaxy are they building here?"

Varek, still simmering with anger over the loss of his marine, leaned against the wall, his eyes filled with fury. "Whatever it is, we'll find out. And when we do, that smug officer's going to pay."

Jax nodded but remained focused on the bigger picture. The intelligence officer had made a tactical error, and time was slipping away to turn it to their advantage. They needed to escape and get the Empire's hands on whatever Black Book Station was hiding—before the Wraiths or, worse, the Intelligence Division itself used it to tip the balance of power.

Jax knew intelligence types too well—they always had their own hidden agendas. To him, it seemed they rarely had the Empire's best interests at heart and operated with minimal oversight. Add advanced tech to that mix, and it was a recipe for disaster.

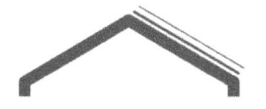

Chapter 41: Tense Situation

The intelligence officer stood beyond the shimmering blue forcefield that confined Dalen, Jax, Rafe, Varek, and the surviving marine. His expression was controlled, but the tension in the air was palpable.

"If I release you now," the officer began, his voice carefully measured, "will you and your forces leave the station and the system?"

Dalen's eyes were cold, his answer immediate. "Not a chance in hell."

The officer's expression tightened. "My superior is on his way, Commander. This situation—"

Dalen cut him off, his tone hard as iron. "Release us, and you live. If you don't, I won't stop Varek from tearing you limb from limb when this is over."

Varek cracked his knuckles from the back of the cell, his eyes gleaming with barely restrained rage. The marine beside him shifted slightly, echoing the sentiment in his stance.

Before the officer could respond, the station's alarms blared, casting the room in flashing red lights. He cursed under his breath, barking a quick order to two robotic soldiers nearby. "Stay here. Guard them."

Without another word, he strode out, leaving the team locked in the brig.

Jax turned to Varek, his expression grim. "Stay sharp. I have a feeling company's on its way, and with any luck, it'll be our people."

Outside, a pirate barge slipped into position beside Black Book Station. With precision, the barge extended a metal tube, cutting an entry point into the station's hull. A temporary airlock was fitted over the hole as the barge slipped away. Moments later, an Imperial shuttle docked, replacing the barge by the airlock, and a marine commando team boarded the station.

The marines moved like shadows through the station's underbelly, their black armor blending into the dimly lit corridors. These were no ordinary troops; each wore an advanced tactical suit optimized for silent movement and swift, lethal breaching. At the head of the team, Captain Morek signaled to a sealed bulkhead ahead.

"Charges," he ordered, his voice low but firm.

A demolitions expert moved forward, setting a series of micro-explosives around the door's frame. With a muffled blast, the door gave way, and the team moved through in perfect formation, weapons raised.

They made quick work of the station's standard defenses, advancing with practiced efficiency. But soon, they encountered a formidable obstacle: robotic soldiers clad in Imperial Intelligence uniforms, moving with deadly precision and efficiency. These machines were faster, more advanced, and equipped with sophisticated weaponry.

A firefight erupted in a storm of plasma blasts and kinetic rounds, the sound echoing through the metal corridors. The marines fought with discipline and skill, but the robotic soldiers were no easy targets. Morek ducked behind a corner as plasma bolts seared past him, scorching the wall.

"We need more charges!" he barked, recalculating their strategy.

A commando tossed him a pack of high-yield explosives, and Morek slapped the detonator, sending an explosive wave through the narrow corridor that tore the robotic soldiers apart.

"Move!" he shouted, pushing the team forward.

As they pressed on, they battled through successive waves of robotic defenders, each engagement more intense than the last. They were nearing the station's core now, where their true objective lay hidden. But at the next bulkhead, they faced another obstacle: a bright blue energy shield, humming with a defensive force.

Morek cursed softly. "Can we breach it?"

One of the commandos scanned the shield, tapping his visor. "It's an advanced shield matrix. We don't have the firepower to bring it down."

Morek's jaw clenched. "Then we improvise," he muttered, already calculating the next move.

Back in the brig, the intelligence officer returned, visibly rattled. The blaring alarms hadn't ceased, and his face was pale as he paced in front of the forcefield.

"Marines have boarded the station," he said, his voice urgent. "Call them off, or they'll be killed."

Varek's eyes narrowed dangerously as he stepped forward, his voice a low growl. "If one more marine dies, I'll make you pay for it personally."

The officer flinched at Varek's intensity but quickly left, keeping the forcefield in place.

Outside the station, Cassian tracked the marines' progress from his cockpit, his gaze flicking between readings. They were advancing but facing stiffer resistance than anticipated.

Suddenly, Cassian's comm board lit up with an incoming message. The frequency was unfamiliar, and it was audio-only. He frowned as he answered.

"Who is this?" Cassian demanded.

A familiar voice came over the speakers, calm and unflappable. "It's Vigil."

Cassian's eyes widened in surprise. "Vigil? What are you doing here?"

"There's no time for details," Vigil replied smoothly. "You need to withdraw the marines from Black Book Station. I'll get Jax and the others out."

Cassian hesitated. "Why should I trust you? What's your angle?"

Vigil's tone remained steady. "Trust me, Cassian. If this assault continues, it will end badly. Let me handle this. Once Dalen and the others are out, convince Dalen to retreat. All will be revealed in time, but for now, let me work."

Before Cassian could press further, the comm cut off abruptly. A moment later, sensors across the battlefield lit up as a small, barely detectable stealth ship jumped into the system.

Cassian's comm buzzed with reports from Imperial and Wraith ships, all reacting to the mysterious vessel.

He keyed the comm again, issuing an urgent order. "Hold positions. Do not engage that ship."

He watched as Vigil's craft approached Black Book Station, slipping past the defensive screens with practiced ease. The ship moved with eerie precision, avoiding detection until it was nearly on top of them. Within moments, it docked in the hangar where Dalen's shuttle was stationed.

Inside the hangar, the massive doors creaked open just enough for Vigil's craft to slip through. Vigil input a command override, sealing the doors behind him. The ship landed with a soft thud, and the hangar was quiet once more.

Vigil moved quickly, interfacing his ship's systems with the station's. He knew time was running out.

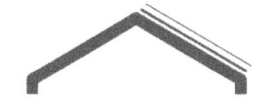

Chapter 42: The Return Of Vigil

Moving through the dark corridors of Black Book Station, Vigil was a ghost. His advanced armor blended seamlessly with the shadows, the suit's adaptive camo shimmering slightly, rendering him nearly invisible. His HUD was alive with warnings and system alerts, but he dismissed them. His singular goal was clear: reach the brig and secure Jax, Dalen, Rafe, Varek, and the marine.

The station's defenses were formidable, yet Vigil's armor was even more advanced. As he approached the brig, his suit tapped into the station's surveillance network, displaying a live feed of the two robotic sentries guarding the prisoners. He keyed in a command to remotely disable them, but a flashing error message quickly alerted him that the system override had failed.

A sigh escaped his lips. "Looks like I'll have to do this the hard way."

From his belt, Vigil withdrew a small cylindrical device. With a press of a stud, a gleaming, razor-sharp blade extended, reflecting the dim corridor lights in an unnatural shimmer. This was no ordinary weapon; it was a high-precision tool, designed for cutting through even the hardest materials.

Vigil moved to the door of the brig and slid it open, entering silently. The robotic guards barely registered his presence before he was upon them. His movements were a blur, too fast for their enhanced reflexes to follow. In a fluid arc, Vigil sliced through the necks of both sentries. Their heads hit the ground with a metallic thud, sparks flying as their systems powered down.

Inside the cell, Jax blinked in surprise, then recognition dawned on his face. "It's Vigil," he muttered to Dalen.

Without delay, Vigil deactivated the forcefield. Dalen, still cautious, stepped forward.

"We're heading to the hangar. You need to leave the station and vacate the system immediately," Vigil said, his voice low and urgent.

Dalen's expression darkened. "Not happening. We haven't even scratched the surface of what's going on here."

Vigil's gaze was intense. "You don't understand. For the Empire's survival, you need to leave now."

The quiet gravity in Vigil's tone gave Dalen pause. After a brief but tense moment, Dalen finally nodded, though reluctance etched his features.

"All right. For now."

Vigil didn't waste another second, leading them swiftly through the maze-like corridors. The team moved with him in silence, encountering no further resistance. They reached the hangar without incident, but Vigil's senses remained heightened, fully aware of the threats still lurking within the station.

Once inside the hangar, the team boarded their shuttle. Vigil watched them strap in, then input a command into his gauntlet. The hangar doors slid open just enough for the shuttle to exit, sealing shut behind it as soon as it cleared.

Without another word, Vigil turned and disappeared back into the station's depths.

Outside, Cassian's sensors picked up the departing shuttle, and he quickly hailed it on an encrypted channel.

"Dalen, this is Cassian. Vigil says you need to leave. Now."

Dalen's voice came through, laced with frustration. "He told me the same. This whole setup stinks, but we're pulling out. We'll regroup and assess."

Cassian held back a sigh. "The commando team is withdrawing—they should be clear in five minutes."

"Understood," Dalen responded. "Once they're out, all units are to rendezvous at Ally Station."

Meanwhile, Vigil made his way through the station's inner corridors, heading toward the intelligence officer's office. His HUD alerted him to several robotic guards stationed outside the door, but he was prepared.

The guards, four in total, were heavily armed and equipped with advanced targeting systems. For most, a direct assault would be suicide, but Vigil was no ordinary operative.

With a flick of his wrist, he activated his blade and charged the first guard. Moving with deadly precision, he drove his blade upward, slicing through the torso of the nearest robot. The second and third guards turned on him, firing a barrage of energy blasts, but he dodged with inhuman speed, deflecting several shots back with his blade, which shorted out their systems.

The final guard fired in quick succession, but Vigil slid low to the ground, avoiding the shots before leaping up, driving his blade into the robot's chest and twisting sharply. The guard collapsed, its systems dead.

Vigil stood among the remnants of the robotic guards, his armor unscathed, glinting faintly in the dim light.

He approached the sealed door to the intelligence officer's office, entering commands on his gauntlet. The door slid open, and Vigil stepped inside. The intelligence officer was waiting, a blaster rifle in hand, and fired a three-round burst directly at Vigil. The shots struck Vigil's armor but barely left a mark.

In a swift motion, Vigil closed the distance, ripping the rifle from the officer's hands. He swung it in a brutal arc, striking the officer across the head and sending him stumbling.

The officer groaned, clutching his head, but he managed to glare up at Vigil, fear mixed with anger in his eyes. "Who are you? What do you think you're doing?"

"Who I am isn't important," Vigil replied.

He loomed over the officer, his voice low and unyielding. "Black Book Station is shutting down."

The officer's expression twisted in desperation. "What about the research? The prototypes—?"

"You were playing with fire," Vigil interrupted, his tone chilling. "You're fortunate I stepped in. Otherwise, today would have marked the beginning of the end for the Steele Empire."

The officer opened his mouth to protest, but Vigil's hard gaze silenced him. Whatever argument he had died in his throat as Vigil stepped back, ensuring the officer understood the gravity of his mistake.

Chapter 43: That's No Moon

Back on Ally Station, Commander Dalen had Cassian and Jax meet him in the pilots' lounge just outside the docking ring. Once they arrived, Dalen gave Cassian a measuring look.

"Cassian, what exactly do you know about this Vigil?" Dalen asked.

"Sir, I've put everything I know in my mission logs," Cassian replied.

Dalen nodded, but let out a heavy sigh. "I know, son, but is there anything you might have left out?"

Cassian shook his head. "No, sir. I haven't held anything back."

Dalen stood, placing a hand on Cassian's shoulder. "He's an unknown quantity. I don't like unknowns."

"Me either, sir," Cassian said, then walked out of the room.

Dalen looked at Jax, raising an eyebrow. "What's your take on Vigil?"

"I don't trust him, sir. We don't know who he is or who he's working for," Jax responded without hesitation.

"Well, nothing to be done about it right now," Dalen said. "Get some sleep. A recon flight from Gaia Prime is due back in the morning. We'll go over their findings in the main briefing room."

With that, the two men made their way back to their quarters.

The briefing room was tense the next morning, shadows cast across the holo-maps of Gaia Prime as Dalen, Jax, and Barlow sifted through the latest scout reports and visual logs. The stalemate continued; Nexus forces surrounded the planet, their massive ships holding an unbreakable formation. The planetary shield held, but for how long was anyone's guess.

Jax's eyes scanned the reports, then something on the holo-display caught his attention. A large, spherical ship hovered over Gaia Prime's northern pole, an ominous presence unlike anything he'd seen in previous logs.

"What's that?" Jax pointed at the ship. "I haven't seen this before."

Barlow leaned in, narrowing his eyes. "That's new. Looks like a command ship. If I were Nexus, I'd use something like that to coordinate my forces."

Jax frowned, considering the possibilities. "What if we take it out? Could that disrupt their fleet, maybe even deactivate the drones?"

Dalen, ever pragmatic, shook his head. "The Nexus ships were already operating long before this sphere appeared. We can't assume it's a silver bullet."

Jax leaned back, thoughtful. "Maybe it wouldn't stop them all, but it could slow them down or throw them off balance. Either way, we need better intel. I'll take Rafe and do a recon run on that ship, get detailed sensor readings."

Dalen's brows furrowed in concern. "Jax, that's risky. These ships have advanced detection systems. Even with Shadow-Class fighters, we're not invisible."

"I know. But we don't have a choice. We need to know what we're up against."

After a moment's pause, Dalen nodded reluctantly. "Fine. But get in and get out. Don't push your luck."

Jax found Rafe in the hangar, prepping his Shadow-Class fighter. The smaller recon craft gleamed under the lights, its sleek design built for speed and stealth rather than heavy firepower or armor.

"We're taking these to Gaia Prime," Jax said as he approached. "That spherical ship—it's new, and we need to find out what it is."

Rafe smirked, clearly eager for the challenge. "Recon run, huh? Sounds easy enough."

"Let's hope it stays that way," Jax replied, fully aware that it rarely did.

The two suited up and boarded their Shadow-Class fighters. Their ships slid out of the hangar bay like wraiths, engines whisper-quiet as they executed a series of randomized jumps to prevent Nexus from tracking them back to Ally Station. After the final jump, they arrived at the edge of the Gaia Prime system.

Activating their stealth systems, they got a firsthand look at the scale of the Nexus fleet. Hundreds of ships orbited Gaia Prime in a massive armada, their dark, sleek shapes exuding menace. Jax's heart sank; the reports hadn't conveyed the sheer enormity of the force before them.

"Looks worse than I thought," Rafe said over the comm.

"Just stay close," Jax replied. "Let's see what we can find before they notice us."

Navigating through the shadows of space, they approached Gaia Prime's northern pole. But as they neared the spherical ship, alarms blared inside their cockpits.

"Damn it!" Jax cursed. "We've been made!"

"Stealth systems compromised," Rafe said, his voice tense. "We've got incoming!"

Nexus forces reacted immediately, swarming toward the two recon fighters like a disturbed hive. Jax and Rafe dove into evasive maneuvers, hands flying over the controls as their ships darted and twisted through the oncoming drones. The Shadow-Class fighters were fast and agile, but their light armaments left them vulnerable in prolonged engagements.

Jax pulled hard to the right, dodging a burst of energy fire from a Nexus drone. He fired off a quick burst from his laser cannons, grazing the shields of the nearest drone, but it wasn't enough to deter their pursuers.

"We're outgunned!" Rafe shouted. "We need to get out—now!"

"I'm working on it!" Jax replied, glancing at his nav console as it calculated the nearest jump point. But with drones closing in from all sides, escape was becoming increasingly difficult.

Suddenly, a shot from one of the Nexus ships hit Jax's fighter directly. His console flickered, emergency lights flashing as smoke began filling the cockpit.

"I'm hit!" Jax yelled, struggling to regain control of his ship. "Rafe, cover me!"

"I've got you," Rafe called back, his fighter swooping in with suppressing fire, giving Jax the critical seconds he needed to reset his systems.

Jax impatiently watched as his systems began coming online, one by one. When they were finally reset, he jabbed the button that would send his fighter hurtling to lightspeed, away from the fleet of Nexus ships. Rafe quickly followed him.

That made a quick jump away from Gaia Prime. They each took a moment to catch their breath.

"We're not getting anywhere near that sphere again," Jax said grimly. "Not without something stronger than just stealth tech."

As they limped back to Ally Station, taking a randomized route to evade any potential pursuit, Dalen met them in the hangar, arms crossed.

"We couldn't get close," Jax said, stepping out of his damaged fighter. "Their detection systems are too advanced. Stealth alone isn't enough."

Dalen let out a long sigh. "Then it's time we pay another visit to Black Book Station. We need something more."

The thought sent a chill down Jax's spine, but he knew Dalen was right. Whatever was hidden within Black Book Station, they were about to find out.

Chapter 44: Detailed Sensor Scans

Jax and Dalen stood at the front of the bridge on the Imperial carrier *SSV McIvey* as it emerged from the ethereal glow of hyperspace into realspace. They expected to see the dark, looming structure of Black Book Station, but instead, they faced a silent field of debris. Fragments of the once-mysterious station drifted in a cold, quiet cloud, illuminated only by the distant starlight.

"What the hell happened?" Jax muttered, his voice tight with disbelief.

Dalen crossed his arms, his expression controlled, though his eyes betrayed a flicker of unease. "Could this be Vigil's doing?"

Jax clenched his jaw, recalling Vigil's cryptic warnings and how he always seemed to be a step ahead. "If it is, he's not telling us everything. He never does."

A voice broke their thoughts. "Sir, we're detecting a communications buoy just outside the debris field," the communications officer reported. "It has a voice-print lock—registered to Cassian."

Jax and Dalen exchanged glances, and Jax sighed. "Call Cassian up from the hangar."

Moments later, Cassian arrived on the bridge, still in his flight suit, his expression darkening as he took in the situation. "This has to be from Vigil," he said, his tone grim.

Dalen nodded toward the ready room at the rear of the bridge. "You should access it in there."

The ready room was dimly lit, and Cassian felt the weight of the moment as he approached the terminal. Keying in his identification, he watched as the holographic image of Vigil appeared, standing tall and as enigmatic as ever.

"Cassian," Vigil's voice was steady but urgent. "Black Book Station was the product of multiple time variances. It was never meant to exist here, and nothing good would have come from it. That's why it's been destroyed."

"They were collecting tech from an alternate Bringi and reverse engineering it," Vigil continued. "It would've led to disaster—one the Empire couldn't survive."

Cassian's heart pounded, though he kept his expression neutral.

Vigil went on. "I'm aware of the spherical ship over Gaia Prime. It doesn't belong in this reality either. It's a threat unlike anything you've faced."

Vigil paused, his gaze locking onto Cassian as if he could see him through the hologram. "But you can't defeat it without proper intel. I'm providing you with detailed scans of the ship."

Cassian felt a measure of relief, but Vigil's next words tempered it. "Be careful, Cassian. I won't always be there to save you." With that, the hologram flickered out, leaving Cassian alone in the dim room.

Cassian lingered, processing Vigil's words. Even with the data, he felt as if he were just a pawn in a larger game. He left the ready room and returned to the bridge, where Jax and Dalen waited.

"Well?" Jax asked.

Cassian recounted Vigil's message, ending with the part about the scans. Dalen's face brightened slightly with hope. "That's a hell of a break. If these scans are accurate, we might finally have a way to take that ship out."

Jax, however, was skeptical. "I don't like this. Vigil knows too much, and he's still pulling the strings from the shadows. There was something on that station he didn't want us to see."

Dalen shrugged. "I don't care. Black Book was a liability, and now it's gone. That's one less problem for us to worry about."

Still uneasy, Jax let the matter drop—for now.

The *McIvey* returned to Ally Station, and soon after, Dalen, Jax, Rafe, and Barlow gathered in the briefing room. Rafe projected the detailed scans of the spherical ship provided by Vigil. The massive vessel hovered ominously in the hologram, its dark, alien design casting a chill over the room.

"This thing... I've never seen anything like it," Rafe began. "It has multiple self-contained shield generators, hundreds of gun emplacements, and armor made from an unknown material. It's completely alien. Even its sensors operate on frequencies far beyond our current tech."

Jax leaned forward, frowning. "So, how do we take it out?"

Rafe shook his head, studying the data. "I'll need time to go through these scans. There might be weaknesses, but nothing's obvious at first glance. I'll keep working."

As Rafe continued analyzing the data, Dalen and Barlow turned their focus to the broader strategic situation. "We need to mobilize," Barlow said. "If we're going to strike, we need to make sure our fleets are ready."

Dalen agreed. "The time to engage the Nexus fleet is coming. We've waited long enough."

Meanwhile, down in the hangar, Cassian stood near his fighter, staring off into the distance, lost in thought. The weight of Vigil's words and the larger scheme he couldn't quite grasp bore down on him, making him feel small—like a cog in a machine beyond his control.

"Hey," came a familiar voice. Cassian looked up to see Bringi approaching with a soft smile. She sat down beside him on a crate, her gaze warm.

"You okay?" she asked, though it was clear she already knew the answer.

Cassian sighed, running a hand through his hair. "I hate it. Being part of a bigger picture but never knowing what the picture is. That's Vigil's game. He pulls us in but leaves us in the dark. It's... frustrating."

Bringi placed a gentle hand on his arm, squeezing. "I know it's hard. But I'm here for you, Cassian. You're not in this alone."

Her words soothed some of the tension inside him. He leaned closer, their foreheads touching. She smiled, brushing her lips softly against his.

Cassian kissed her back, feeling the weight lift slightly. Pulling back, he gave her a mischievous grin. "You know, I can think of something that might take my mind off things for a while."

Bringi laughed, her eyes warm with affection. "Lead the way."

Together, they walked deeper into the hangar, their steps lighter than they had been in days. For a brief moment, the galaxy's problems faded into the background, leaving just the two of them.

Chapter 45: Maximum Carnage Onboard

The Rescue Fleet spent the next several days in intense preparation. Techs and engineers ran diagnostics, made repairs, and reinforced key systems. Armorers loaded ordnance and tested targeting arrays, ensuring each weapon was battle-ready. The capital ships' crews drilled tirelessly, conducting war games to simulate combat scenarios, while the fighter pilots flew training missions for hours on end.

Watching it all, Commander Dalen felt the heavy weight of command. He was leading this makeshift fleet into a battle he wasn't confident they could win. They had prepared as best they could, but he knew that many good men and women would not return. He silently hoped the scans Vigil had supplied would reveal something useful soon; everyone was eager to defend the Empire's capital.

Tension hung in the air, thick and palpable. Then, one day, Rafe's voice crackled over the comms, summoning Jax and Dalen to the briefing room. They exchanged a glance, sensing the urgency in his tone.

When they arrived, they found Rafe hunched over the holo-table, his eyes bloodshot and his uniform wrinkled, as though he hadn't slept in days. Despite his fatigue, his excitement was unmistakable.

Jax took one look at him and shook his head. "Rafe, when was the last time you slept? You look like you've been up for days."

Dalen, always focused on the task at hand, waved the comment off. "Never mind that. Tell us about the weakness."

Rafe nodded eagerly, bringing up the scans of the spherical ship. "The shields... they rotate frequencies. It's how they absorb and deflect damage, and it's why their sensors refresh in real-time. That's why we couldn't get close without being detected. But there's a pattern. The frequencies shift in a predictable sequence. If we match the shield rotation, we can get a single ship through undetected—just long enough."

Jax frowned. "One ship isn't going to be enough against that monster."

Dalen crossed his arms, his brow furrowed. "Not from the outside, no. But if we can get a boarding shuttle inside, loaded with marines, they might be able to disable it from within."

The room fell silent. Jax finally spoke, breaking the tension. "And how do we get the marines out? If we send them in, it's basically a suicide mission."

Dalen sighed, feeling the weight of his command. "I don't like it either, but we're out of options. Let's bring Varek in and see what he thinks."

Moments later, Varek, the grizzled leader of the marine company aboard the *McIvey*, entered the room. His face was hardened, as always, but as he listened to the plan, a spark lit in his eyes—determination or resignation, Dalen couldn't quite tell.

"My marines will do what needs doing," Varek said simply, his gravelly voice steady. Then he raised a brow. "But tell me something. Why don't we just load the shuttle with explosives? Get in, plant the bombs, and get out before they detonate."

Dalen cursed under his breath. It was a painfully simple idea, and he was kicking himself for not thinking of it sooner. "You're right. That's exactly what we should do. Can your ordnance techs put something like that together?"

Varek nodded. "I'll consult with them. We'll need the right materials, but it's doable. I'll get back to you."

An hour later, Varek returned, a grim smile on his face. "The techs say it's possible. We'll build a two-stage bomb. The first stage will be an EMP blast, strong enough to knock out some of their systems. The second stage will be a shielded high-yield warhead. Once the EMP does its job, the warhead goes off, maximizing damage."

Jax let out a low whistle. "That'll do some serious damage. Timed right, it could cripple the whole ship."

"What about the shuttle?" Dalen asked. "Won't the EMP disable it too?"

"Not necessarily," Rafe replied. "If we convert enough of the shuttle to mechanical controls and harden the essential electronics, it should survive the EMP—and be harder to detect."

"Get with the techs and start on a shuttle refit immediately," Jax ordered.

Dalen, looking more hopeful than he had in days, summoned Captain Barlow to the meeting. When Barlow arrived and was briefed on the plan, his response was swift. "Give me a list of what you need. If the Wraiths have it, we'll find it."

For the first time in days, Dalen felt a spark of hope. "All right, Varek. Hand-pick your marines and demo techs. Make sure they're the best. They'll need to escort the bombs deep into that ship."

Varek grunted in affirmation. "Consider it done. We'll make sure the bombs reach their target."

Dalen leaned forward, fingers tapping the edge of the holo-table. "Barlow and I will need to coordinate with our ship commanders. We'll have to create a diversion—keep the Nexus fleet occupied while the shuttle slips through. If they catch on to what we're doing too early, the whole plan falls apart."

Jax, ever the realist, added, "We won't last long against a fleet that size, even with a distraction. They could overwhelm us before we can get the bombs in place."

Dalen's expression was resolute, though doubt flickered in his eyes. "We don't have a choice. If we don't try this, Gaia Prime falls. The Empire falls. It's all or nothing."

Jax leaned back, eyes fixed on the hologram of the spherical ship looming like a dark omen. The stakes had never been higher. Yet, despite everything, Jax couldn't shake a growing suspicion gnawing at him.

"Still," he muttered, almost to himself, "I can't help but wonder if Vigil is pulling the strings. What else does he know that he's not telling us?"

Dalen, too weary for more theories, simply replied, "Let's focus on what we do know. We've got a shot here—more than we had yesterday."

Jax nodded, though his thoughts lingered on Vigil's shadowy influence. They had a plan, but at what cost?

As the meeting ended, the weight of the upcoming mission settled heavily over them all. There was no turning back now. The marines, the fleet—everyone was part of a desperate gamble to save the Empire from an unimaginable threat.

Deep down, Jax knew that whatever happened next, nothing would ever be the same again.

Chapter 46: Calm Before The Storm

Captain Barlow wasted no time. As soon as Varek's techs finalized the list of materials for the bombs, he dispatched a fleet to secure the supplies. The mission was clear, and delays weren't an option. The Wraiths had stashes of advanced tech and explosives scattered across the sector, and Barlow knew exactly where to look. As the ships departed, each crew understood the urgency—the bombs were critical, and they had to be ready fast.

Meanwhile, Barlow and Commander Dalen gathered in the strategy room with the other Rescue Fleet commanders. The holographic map of Gaia Prime and the Nexus fleet surrounding it projected above them, with intel gathered by the Shadow-class fighters offering a clearer picture. Nexus ships were arranged in a tight defensive ring, coordinated to counter any attack.

"Their formation is precise," noted Commander Arlen of the *Vigilant*, gesturing to the hologram, "but they've left a gap here." He pointed to a weaker section of the fleet.

Barlow studied the map. "That's where we'll strike. A feint there will draw their defenses, creating an opening for the marines."

Dalen nodded. "We need to be cautious, though. A portion of our fleet should be ready to pull out fast if things go sideways. We'll hit hard and quick, but our priority is getting Varek's marines inside."

The battle plan was set. As the meeting ended, the commanders dispersed, preparing their crews for the assault.

On Ally Station, an unusual camaraderie formed amid the tension. Jax, Rafe, Cassian, Bringi, and McHenry gathered in a newly opened Wraith-run bar tucked away in a quiet corner. Though once enemies, the Wraiths had seized the lull to set up a place for a drink and respite, and the alliance—built out of necessity—had brought everyone together.

They sat around a small table, nursing drinks that glowed amber under the bar's dim lights. A somber mood filled the air as they remembered those who hadn't made it back.

"To the ones we lost," Jax said, raising his glass. The others followed, clinking their glasses in a solemn toast.

Rafe, still weary from work on the shields, took a long sip. "We've lost too many."

McHenry nodded, staring into his drink. "This war has taken everything from some of us. But we keep fighting."

Cassian, his hand resting on Bringi's knee under the table, glanced at her, feeling the weight of his own thoughts. "Fighting's all we've got."

Bringi leaned into him, sensing his internal conflict. She squeezed his hand silently in support.

They sat in silence, united by their losses and steeling themselves for what lay ahead. War had a way of forging bonds even as it tore people apart.

Elsewhere, Varek's marines gathered in a secluded hangar bay. Varek and his top tech, Sergeant Rykov, walked a tight circle of marines and demo techs through the plan.

"The bombs are two-stage," Rykov explained, projecting a schematic. "EMP first, then high-yield warhead. The EMP will knock out their systems long enough for us to get our shuttle out."

A marine raised his hand. "What if we can't get out?"

Varek's face hardened. "Finish the mission. No matter what."

No one asked further questions; they knew the risks.

"Get some rest," Varek said, his voice gruff. "We go soon."

In his quarters, Dalen sat alone, a glass of whiskey in hand. Command weighed heavier than ever as he stared at a photo of his family on Gaia Prime. His chest tightened with fear; he hadn't told anyone, not even Jax, that his family was on the planet. The risk of losing them gnawed at him.

The whiskey burned as he sipped, trying to numb the worry, but it didn't help. He was their commander, and he had to make the hard decisions, knowing they could cost him everything he held dear.

In the quiet of their quarters, Cassian and Bringi found a moment's peace. They had recently moved in together, and the closeness was a comfort amid the chaos. As they lay together, Cassian's thoughts drifted to the enormity of what was to come.

"I hate not knowing," he murmured, his voice low as he rested his head on Bringi's shoulder. "I feel like I'm part of something bigger, but I don't even know what it is."

Bringi ran her fingers through his hair, soothing him. "I know it's frustrating. But you're not alone in this. I'm here with you, and we'll face whatever comes together."

Cassian looked up at her, eyes filled with gratitude and affection. He leaned in, and for a brief moment, their kiss took them away from the weight of it all.

Far across the galaxy, Vigil stood alone in a dim corridor aboard a Nexus ship, body tense, cloak billowing as advanced robotic soldiers closed in. Their metal limbs clanged against the floor, red eyes locking onto him.

Vigil moved in a blur, his sword slicing through the air. One robot lunged, and he sidestepped, his blade cleaving through it. Sparks flew as it collapsed.

Two more charged. Vigil extended his hand, releasing a pulse of energy that slammed them into the walls. Before they could recover, he was upon them, cutting them down with brutal efficiency.

The final robot, larger than the others, advanced, transforming its arms into blasters. It fired, but Vigil dodged with inhuman grace, closing the gap and driving his sword into its chest. The robot sputtered, red eyes flickering out as it fell.

Breathing heavily, Vigil moved to a terminal, initiating the ship's self-destruct. For a moment, he stared at the screen.

"I wish I could help you, Cassian," he muttered, regret in his voice. "I'm tired of only eliminating the targets I'm assigned. But the rules... I can't interfere."

As the countdown began, Vigil turned, his cloak sweeping behind him as he made his way to the exit. The Nexus ship exploded behind him, reduced to debris in the cold expanse.

For now, Vigil had done his part. But the battle was far from over.

Chapter 47: Battle For Gaia Prime

Barlow, Dalen, Jax, and Varek stood around the holo-table in the briefing room, faces illuminated by the soft blue glow of Gaia Prime and the surrounding Nexus fleet. The tension was thick, and each of them understood the gravity of what was about to unfold.

Varek spoke first, his voice resolute. "The bombs are ready, and my marines are prepped. We've drilled the plan extensively; there won't be any surprises on our end."

Dalen nodded, eyes fixed on the hologram. "Good. Barlow and I have finalized our attack plan for the Rescue Fleet. We'll target the outlying ships, drawing as many Nexus forces away as possible. We'll hit them hard, make them think we're the primary threat."

Barlow adjusted the projection. "Once we engage, Raptor Squadron will escort the marine shuttle. It'll be a tough fight, but the marines need to board the Nexus spherical ship. Once they're inside, we'll hold the line until they signal for extraction."

Jax crossed his arms, studying the ship layouts. "Raptor Squadron's ready. We'll get Varek's marines through, but after that, we'll be in the thick of it. The Nexus won't let us slip away easily."

Dalen sighed. "We have no choice. This has to work."

The next day, tension rippled through the fleet as they prepared for the assault. Ally Station was left with only a skeleton defense, a few gunships and fighters remaining. The rest of the fleet had jumped to the staging area outside the Gaia Prime system.

In the depths of space, the *McIvey* and other ships of the Rescue Fleet hovered like shadows, engines humming as they awaited the order. Then, with a flash, the Wraiths jumped into the system first, launching a surprise attack on a lightly defended section of the Nexus fleet.

The Wraith ships, agile and ruthless, darted through the chaos like wolves among sheep. Caught off guard, Nexus light cruisers and frigates scattered under a barrage of laser fire and torpedoes. Dark-hulled Wraith ships twisted and dodged, exploiting gaps with ruthless precision. Torpedoes streaked through space, detonating against Nexus ships, shields flaring before hulls shattered.

Nexus drones swarmed in response, cold and calculating. Moving in tight formations, they fired with deadly precision, vaporizing several Wraith fighters in flashes of light. Still, the Wraith fleet pressed forward, hammering Nexus defenses. Heavy Wraith gunships focused on a Nexus destroyer, ripping through its shields with ion cannons and missiles until it split apart, debris scattering into the void.

Just as the Wraiths gained the upper hand, a massive wave of Imperial Navy ships jumped into the system. The Rescue Fleet, led by Dalen and Barlow, descended upon the Nexus forces like an avalanche, capital ships bristling with firepower.

"All ships, engage at will!" Dalen's voice echoed over comms as the *McIvey* surged forward.

The Imperial Navy's cruisers and destroyers unleashed devastating broadsides of energy blasts and missiles. A Nexus capital ship, angular and ominous, bore the brunt, its shields flaring before collapsing, its hull torn apart by the Rescue Fleet's guns.

Amid the chaos, Nexus drones and fighters poured out like a relentless swarm, targeting Imperial fighters with tight formations and precision fire. Predator-class starfighters, with superior maneuverability and weaponry, weaved through the onslaught, picking off dozens of drones. Yet, for every drone destroyed, more filled the void, an unending tide.

Jax led Raptor Squadron through the maelstrom, his voice calm but tense over the comms. "Keep it tight. Watch your six; these drones aren't letting up."

Rafe's voice crackled through comms. "They're everywhere, Jax! We're losing ships fast!"

Meanwhile, capital ships from the Rescue Fleet clashed with the Nexus armada. Space lit up with fire from ion cannons, plasma rounds, and missiles.

An Imperial cruiser took a direct hit from a Nexus beam weapon, its shields buckling before the beam punched through, sending it spinning out of control and exploding into a fireball.

Aboard the *McIvey*, Dalen watched the battle unfold, his heart pounding. The Nexus fleet held a firm defensive posture around the spherical ship, refusing to be drawn away. They were disciplined, focused on Gaia Prime, and the plan was on the verge of collapse.

"We can't keep this up!" Jax's voice came over the comms. "We're taking heavy losses!"

Dalen grimaced, preparing to call off the assault when, suddenly, the void lit up. Gaia Prime's surface-to-space cannons roared to life, beams of energy cutting through the darkness, striking Nexus ships. Massive planetary guns fired from behind Gaia Prime's shields, catching several Nexus vessels in their path.

"Gaia Prime's guns are online!" Dalen shouted, a surge of hope in his voice.

The powerful beams sliced through Nexus ships, scattering their formations. With the added pressure from the planet, Nexus forces began to shift, drawing more of their fleet toward the Rescue Fleet to face the combined might of the Wraiths, the Imperial Navy, and Gaia Prime's defenses.

Now, the sky was alive with the fury of battle. Capital ships exchanged brutal firepower, explosions and energy discharges lighting up the void. A Nexus dreadnought released a swarm of drone fighters, overwhelming an Imperial destroyer before the destroyer retaliated with a missile salvo that tore through the drones, ramming its bow into the dreadnought and crippling it.

Predator-class fighters darted through the chaos, engines glowing as they twisted to evade Nexus drones. They strafed enemy ships, picking off drones with precise fire. Cassian, flying alongside Jax, locked onto a Nexus fighter and destroyed it with a well-placed shot.

"This is insane!" Bringi's voice crackled over the comms. "There's too many of them!"

"Just hold on!" Jax replied. "We're almost there."

With the battlefield at its most chaotic, Dalen gave the order. "Jump us in!"

In a flash, the *McIvey* appeared close to the spherical ship. As they moved into position, the launch bay doors opened, and the marine boarding shuttle launched. Raptor Squadron quickly formed up around it, clearing a path through Nexus drones.

Jax took the lead, scanning the battlefield. "Alright, this is it! Stay close, and don't get separated!"

The shuttle, loaded with Varek's marines and the bombs, shot toward the spherical ship. Raptor Squadron flew in tight formation, fending off Nexus drones as they closed in on their target.

The spherical ship loomed ahead, a dark and foreboding presence, bristling with weapons and shield generators. Raptor Squadron faced a grueling final stretch as they protected the shuttle. The mission's outcome—and the fate of Gaia Prime and the Empire—hung in the balance.

Chapter 48: Once A Marine, Always A Marine

The five remaining ships of Raptor Squadron tore through the endless waves of Nexus drones, engines roaring in tight formation. Explosions filled the dark void as drones swarmed the marine shuttle. Jax flew in the lead, his hands steady on the controls, scanning the battlefield as every second counted toward reaching the spherical ship.

"Stay tight!" Jax commanded over the comms. "We've got to get them through!"

The Nexus drones buzzed around them like a swarm of angry hornets, lasers crisscrossing through space. Rafe peeled off to take out a formation of drones targeting the shuttle. His fighter spun and twisted through the chaos, precise shots disabling two drones in quick succession.

"I'm thinning the herd, but they're everywhere!" Rafe called out, his voice tense.

The marine shuttle dodged and weaved through the firestorm, its pilot struggling to match the rotating frequency of the spherical ship's shields. Time was running short.

"We're taking too long!" Jax cursed under his breath. "Rafe, assist the shuttle pilot; we're about to be overwhelmed!"

Rafe swooped close to the shuttle, syncing his fighter's systems to match the shuttle's. With Nexus drones closing in and firing, Rafe's fingers danced over his controls, adjusting the shuttle's shields to align with the rotating frequency of the spherical ship's defenses.

"They're through!" Rafe shouted as the shuttle slipped past the shields.

Inside, the marines braced as they skimmed the spherical ship's surface, locating a wide entry bay on the lower section. Dark and foreboding, the bay door yawned open. With a hiss, the shuttle docked, and Raptor Squadron peeled off, their engines roaring back toward the main battle.

In the shuttle, the marines were prepped for combat, adrenaline charging the air. As the bay doors slid open with a hydraulic hiss, they stormed into the landing bay, boots pounding on the cold metal floor. The hum of the ship's systems filled the space, an ominous reminder of where they were.

Clad in advanced power armor and gripping powerful pulse blaster rifles, the marines moved like a wall of steel around the techs pushing hover sleds loaded with the bombs.

"Move, move, move!" Sergeant Varek's voice boomed as the first squad disembarked, rifles at the ready.

Without warning, robotic soldiers emerged from the shadows, red optics flaring to life as they opened fire. The marines ducked behind crates and support beams, their pulse rifles roaring back. The air thickened with the crackle of energy blasts and the boom of grenades. Varek's team returned fire with precise bursts, but the robotic soldiers advanced in flawless formation, impervious to standard rounds.

"EMP rounds, now!" Varek shouted.

Several marines adjusted their rifles, switching to EMP rounds that hit the robotic soldiers dead center, frying their circuits instantly. The robots collapsed, sparking and twitching, but more poured in, their metallic footsteps echoing as they pushed forward.

"Push forward!" Varek ordered, his voice gritted as he fired round after round into the mechanical ranks.

A brutal firefight ensued, the bay filled with the stench of ozone and burning circuitry. The marines held their ground, taking down robotic soldiers one by one. Sparks flew, grenades erupted in blinding flashes, and shattered bits of metal scattered across the floor. By the time the smoke cleared, the bay was secured. But Varek had lost men.

He wiped the sweat from his brow, signaling to the techs. "Techs, bring the bombs!"

With swift efficiency, the demolition techs rolled the hover sleds forward, making final checks on the bombs. Varek led them deeper into the ship's labyrinthine corridors. The ship vibrated beneath their feet, a constant reminder that the battle outside still raged.

At each turn, they faced chokepoints crowded with more robotic soldiers. The marines were forced to adapt quickly as the enemy pressed on, firing relentlessly. The firefights intensified, leaving scorch marks along the walls and littering the floor with smoldering debris. Varek lost more marines with every advance, their bodies falling in the barrage of robotic fire. Those who survived wore grim expressions as they pressed forward, undeterred.

"We're almost there!" one of the techs shouted over the comms as they reached a massive, shielded door.

Beyond lay the ship's core, a towering construct pulsing with raw energy. The techs moved swiftly, setting the final bomb next to the core and working the wiring with focused intensity.

Suddenly, a door hissed open behind them. More robotic soldiers poured into the room, catching the marines off guard. Varek barked orders, throwing himself into the fray as the marines opened fire, pulse blasters rattling with deadly precision. But the sheer numbers pressed them back, lasers slicing through the air.

A shot pierced Varek's side, pain exploding through his body. Staggering, he gritted his teeth, pushing past the agony to continue firing. The marines fought ferociously, forcing the robotic soldiers back with everything they had. After what felt like an eternity, the final robotic soldier collapsed, sparks and smoke leaking from its shattered chassis.

Varek dropped to one knee, clutching his side as blood poured from the wound, soaking through his armor. His vision blurred, but he was pulled back to focus as one of the techs rushed over, panic evident in his eyes.

"Sergeant, the detonator's damaged!" the tech exclaimed. "The remote won't work. The only way to set it off is manually."

Varek's face hardened as he realized what it meant. He looked at his remaining marines, their faces pale as they comprehended the situation.

"You know what has to be done," Varek rasped, voice thick with pain and resolve. "I'll stay behind. You all get back to the shuttle."

"Sir, no!" one of the marines protested. "We're not leaving you!"

Varek shook his head, grimacing as the pain flared. "You will. I'm not making it out anyway." He turned to the tech. "Show me how to manually detonate this thing."

The tech hesitated but quickly showed Varek the sequence, explaining each button and step. The marines stood around, torn between their duty and their loyalty to him.

"Go," Varek commanded, his tone leaving no room for argument. "That's an order."

Reluctantly, the remaining marines and techs retreated, casting a final look back before disappearing into the corridor.

Leaning heavily against the bomb, Varek felt his strength fading with each breath, blood pooling at his feet. He knew his time was short, but he found solace in knowing the mission would be completed.

As his vision dimmed, he whispered, "It's been a hell of a ride."

With a shaking hand, he reached for the detonator and prepared to make his final stand.

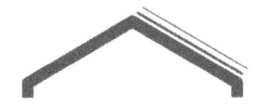

Chapter 49: This Is Our Moment

Jax gripped the controls of his starfighter, his palms sweaty despite the cool air circulating through the cockpit. Raptor Squadron had been locked in combat for what felt like days, battling wave after wave of Nexus drones as they tore through the chaos above Gaia Prime. Each pilot was at their limit, their reflexes frayed by exhaustion, when the call came through, just as they thought they couldn't push any further.

"The marine shuttle is ready to depart," crackled the comms from the *McIvey*, the signal jolting them back to attention.

Jax straightened, quickly wiping the sweat from his brow. "Raptor Squadron, form up! We've got to get our marines out of there. This is it!"

They cut through the battlefield, maneuvering through the dense chaos of energy blasts and flares. The sheer scale of the Nexus fleet was staggering, dark shapes blotting out the stars as they encircled Gaia Prime. Below, surface-to-space guns roared to life, massive beams of energy blasting upward to aid the Imperial fleet.

"Stay sharp, everyone," Jax said, feeling the weight of the battle pressing down on him and his squadron.

Ahead, the marine shuttle shot out from the docking bay of the massive Nexus spherical ship, engines blazing as it sped toward safety. But the Nexus drones weren't done yet. Another wave closed in on the shuttle, a lethal swarm determined to intercept before it could escape.

"Here they come!" Rafe's strained voice broke through the comms.

Jax rolled his fighter into position, leading the charge. Blaster fire erupted around them, as Raptor Squadron tore into the drones, forming a defensive perimeter around the shuttle. The pilots pushed their battle-worn ships to the limit, evading incoming fire while fighting to keep the relentless drones from overwhelming their marines.

Raptor Squadron and the drone swarm clashed in a deadly display of precision and firepower, a testament to why they had earned their reputation as one of the Empire's finest. Bright laser blasts sliced through the dark, and missile trails streaked across the void, each hit lighting up space in violent flashes.

"Hold the line!" Jax commanded, his hands steady despite the storm of fire around them. "We've got to get them home!"

One by one, Raptor Squadron's ships cut down drones, finally creating an escape corridor for the shuttle. The shuttle's engines flared as it broke for the *McIvey*, Raptor Squadron right on its tail, keeping the remaining drones at bay.

With a final burst of speed, the shuttle glided into the *McIvey*'s docking bay. Raptor Squadron circled back, clearing the hangar of any remaining threats before reforming.

"Shuttle secured," came the calm voice from the *McIvey*. Relief surged through Jax, though it was short-lived.

Suddenly, a bright flash caught his attention. From across the battlefield, explosions erupted from the spherical ship, cascading outward in a violent wave of destruction. The vessel's core shattered, unleashing a chain reaction that blasted through its superstructure. Flames and debris shot into space as the once-mighty vessel began to deform, huge chunks breaking away from its hull.

"By the stars..." Rafe murmured, awe filling his voice as he watched the ship's destruction ripple outward.

The spherical ship drifted away from Gaia Prime, the wreckage spilling out like a slow-motion firework display. Massive sections detached, and within moments, the ship was nothing more than a floating graveyard.

Then, an unexpected shift occurred. Nexus drones throughout the battlefield began to falter, going limp and drifting aimlessly as if a switch had been flipped. Larger Nexus vessels lost power, listing and drifting without direction. Those drones and ships that remained active now moved erratically, devoid of the precision and coordination that had once made them so formidable.

"This is our moment!" Jax called out over the comms, adrenaline sparking his voice. "Let's finish this!"

Raptor Squadron dove back into the fight, invigorated by the sight of the crumbling enemy. The Rescue Fleet pressed forward, Imperial warships unleashing full salvos at the now-disorganized Nexus ships. Capital ships exchanged punishing volleys, shields flickering as turbolasers and plasma beams slammed into armor plating. The *McIvey*, charging forward, scored a direct hit on a Nexus dreadnought, its hull splitting apart in a fiery explosion that sent shockwaves across the battlefield.

Fighter squadrons tangled with the remaining drones, Imperial pilots moving with renewed intensity. Jax's squadron executed flawless maneuvers, picking off Nexus drones that were now easy prey. Rafe's fighter barrel-rolled through the debris, taking out two drones with a perfectly timed burst, while Cassian and Bringi weaved between enemy ships, expertly exploiting the gaps in the Nexus formation.

"Don't let any of them escape!" Dalen's commanding voice echoed over the comms, steely and determined. "All Nexus ships must be destroyed! Keep them within the planet's gravity well so they can't jump away!"

Despite the lack of coordination, several large Nexus vessels still posed a formidable threat, stubbornly resisting as they exchanged fire with Imperial capital ships. The *McIvey* and her escorts zeroed in, unleashing devastating broadsides that tore through the remaining Nexus hulls. The planetary guns from Gaia Prime hammered the survivors, preventing any chance of escape.

Desperate, the largest Nexus ships tried to break away, pushing outward in an attempt to reach safe distance for a jump to lightspeed. But the Imperial fleet surrounded them at every turn, relentlessly targeting the retreating vessels. Explosions filled the void as Nexus battleships were caught in the relentless crossfire, torn apart piece by piece under the combined might of the Rescue Fleet and Gaia Prime's defense guns.

Amidst the chaos, Raptor Squadron cut through the last of the drones. Exhaustion gripped each pilot, but as the final Nexus ships were vaporized by concentrated Imperial fire, a grim sense of satisfaction washed over them.

Finally, after what felt like an eternity, the last Nexus ship disintegrated in a brilliant explosion, scattering fiery debris into the silent void.

Jax leaned back in his seat, breathing heavily, allowing himself a moment of relief. "We did it," he whispered, the weight of victory settling over him.

As the echoes of the battle faded, a message beamed out across all Imperial channels. Emperor Landon Steele's voice, steady and filled with emotion, resonated through the comms. His image flickered across every display, reaching every corner of the fleet.

"To the brave men and women of Rescue Fleet," he began, his voice calm but powerful. "You have my eternal gratitude. Gaia Prime, and the Empire, owe their very existence to your courage and sacrifice. Though the Empire has been battered, thanks to your efforts, it remains very much alive."

A pause hung in the air, and his gaze turned steely with determination. "The Nexus sought to destroy us, but today, we stand victorious. The Steele Empire will rise again, stronger than ever."

The message ended, but the impact lingered, echoing in the hearts of everyone who had fought. The Battle for Gaia Prime was over. The Empire had emerged, bruised and bloodied, but unbroken.

In the quiet that followed, Jax looked out over the debris field—the shattered remnants of the Nexus fleet drifting, lifeless, in space. They had paid a heavy price, but they had won. Gaia Prime was safe, and with it, the Steele Empire's future still burned bright.

Chapter 50: An Audience With The Emperor

The sky above Gaia Prime stretched in a deep, endless blue, as if the heavens themselves were honoring the day's events. Dalen, Jax, Cassian, Bringi, McHenry, and Rafe stood outside the Emperor's Palace, each in gleaming dress uniforms that caught the sunlight. Behind them, the palace loomed, its marble and gold facade a testament to the Empire's former grandeur. But as they waited for their audience with the Emperor, a nervous tension rippled through the group.

"I'll be damned," Rafe muttered, eyes widening as another sleek shuttle touched down nearby. The shuttle door hissed open, and Captain Barlow stepped out. Despite his unkempt hair and scruffy beard, he wore a surprisingly clean coat—a rare sight.

"Captain Barlow," Jax greeted with a smirk, nodding at the rogue-turned-ally. "Didn't expect to see you so... polished."

Barlow shrugged, a glint of humor in his eyes. "Well, the invitation said formal attire. Figured it wouldn't kill me for one day, though I think the Emperor's Guard was less than thrilled about it."

Dalen chuckled as they shared quick greetings, the camaraderie easing the tension for a moment. But soon enough, the towering palace doors creaked open, and a line of Imperial guards appeared, ushering them inside. They passed through grand hallways, their footsteps echoing faintly in vast chambers adorned with priceless artwork and gilded columns. Every detail reflected the Empire's resilience, its majesty weathered but undiminished.

At last, they reached the throne room. Emperor Landon Steele awaited them, his presence commanding in the center of the room, clad in regal attire that symbolized the enduring power of the Steele line. As they approached, everyone but Barlow knelt in reverence.

"Rise," the Emperor said, his voice warm but undeniably powerful.

They rose to their feet, and the Emperor's gaze settled on Barlow, a faint smile tugging at his lips. "Captain Barlow," he began, "the Empire owes you and the Wraiths a considerable debt. You could have turned away, yet you chose to stand with us. How might the Empire repay that debt?"

Barlow stepped forward, clearly having prepared for this moment. "Well, Your Majesty," he replied, scratching his beard, "the Wraiths would like to have our borders officially recognized. We want to be acknowledged as a sovereign state, allied but separate from the Empire."

The Emperor's smile deepened, his eyes gleaming with a hint of knowing. "I expected as much. But be aware, Captain: leading a nation is a far different task than commanding a crew of pirates."

Barlow nodded. "I know. There'll be growing pains for sure, but we'll make it work."

Satisfied, the Emperor turned his attention to Dalen, his expression turning solemn. "Admiral Dalen," he began, and Dalen blinked, caught off guard by the new title. "The Imperial Fleet has been decimated, and rebuilding it is our top priority. I can think of no one more suited to oversee that effort. Therefore, I am promoting you to Admiral and making you Chief of Naval Operations."

Dalen's composure wavered, his throat tight with emotion. "Thank you, Your Majesty. I won't let you down."

With a nod, the Emperor addressed Jax. "Now, to Raptor Squadron. Your team was indispensable, both in the Battle of Gaia Prime and in the weeks leading up to it. Midway Station will be rebuilt, and I would like you, Commander Ryland, to become its new commander. As for the rest of Raptor Squadron, I intend for each of you to lead a squadron of your own. And Lieutenant Rafe, there is a position awaiting you in Imperial Intelligence."

Though deeply honored, Jax took a steadying breath before responding. "Your Majesty, with respect, may I make a request?"

Intrigued, the Emperor raised an eyebrow. "Go ahead, Commander. You've earned the right."

Jax glanced at his teammates, his resolve clear. "I'd like command of the *McIvey*, and I'd like Lieutenant Gray to take over Raptor Squadron. We've become more than a team—we're a family."

The Emperor considered Jax's proposal for a long moment, his gaze sweeping over the group. Finally, he smiled. "Your squadron is indeed something special. That's a grand idea. Assuming the rest of you agree?"

Each member of Raptor Squadron voiced their excitement and agreement, the bonds forged in battle evident in their shared determination.

Dalen, curious at the mention of Imperial Intelligence, took a step forward. "Since Intelligence has been brought up, Your Majesty, there are questions I've been meaning to ask, particularly about Black Book Station."

The Emperor's expression darkened slightly, though there was no malice. "In due time, Admiral. For now, let us celebrate what has been achieved." The cryptic response left Dalen intrigued, a reminder that mysteries still lingered within the Empire.

Later that evening, they gathered in a grand hall for a feast in their honor. The long tables overflowed with food and drink, and the lively hum of laughter and conversation filled the air. Barlow, visibly more relaxed, joked about his future as the President of the Wraith Nation, drawing laughter from his Imperial allies.

Jax stood, raising his glass. "A toast," he called, and the room quieted. "To the Rescue Fleet and everything we've accomplished. To the battles we've fought and those we've lost. We wouldn't be here without them."

A resounding cheer erupted, glasses clinking as they celebrated not only victory but survival. Moments later, Cassian cleared his throat, standing with Bringi beside him, drawing curious looks.

"I have an announcement," Cassian said, his voice carrying a quiet intensity. He lifted Bringi's hand, revealing a gleaming engagement ring.

The hall filled with applause and cheers, louder than ever. Bringi blushed, her smile radiant as Cassian wrapped his arm around her waist, sharing a private moment amidst the celebration.

"To the betrothed couple!" Dalen bellowed, lifting his glass high. Everyone joined, their joy infectious.

As the night wore on, laughter and stories flowed freely, deepening the bonds they had forged in battle. Though the war had cost them dearly, they had emerged together, and the Empire still had a future.

Watching from afar, Emperor Landon Steele allowed a proud smile to touch his lips. The Empire had been brought back from the brink, and it was these brave souls who had made it possible.

Prologue

Cassian stood on the observation deck of the newly completed Imperial shipyards, constructed in orbit above Gaia Prime. Through the viewport, he watched the *McIvey*, which was undergoing the final stages of a full refit. Admiral Dalen had made upgrading the battered vessels of the former Rescue Fleet—now known as the First Home Fleet—a priority. Cassian knew that soon all the ships would be like new, and after that, the shipyards would begin constructing new vessels to rebuild the Navy decimated by the war with Nexus forces.

As Cassian studied the view, he sensed someone behind him and jumped slightly.

"Cassian," a distorted voice greeted him.

He turned, hiding his surprise, and found himself facing the enigmatic figure of Vigil. Embarrassed to have been caught off guard, he tried to brush it off. "I'd ask how you got in here, but I know better," Cassian quipped, only half-joking.

Vigil nodded, his gaze shifting to the *McIvey* through the viewport. "She's a fine ship."

"She's our home," Cassian replied with a proud nod.

"And she will be for some time yet," Vigil added cryptically.

Cassian sighed, turning back to the scene outside. "I know you have answers, Vigil, but you always seem to have more mysteries too," he said, a hint of frustration in his voice.

Vigil's tone grew serious. "Cassian, I understand your frustration. I can't answer everything, but my time here is done. I've come to give you what answers I can."

Then Vigil did something Cassian never expected. Raising both hands, he unsealed his helmet. With a faint hiss of escaping air, Vigil lifted it off, revealing his face. Cassian's eyes widened as he looked into a scarred, older version of himself.

For a moment, words failed him. Finally, he managed, "I guess I shouldn't be surprised, should I?"

"Like the other Bringi, I'm from the future, but not *your* future," Vigil explained calmly. "I was sent here, from an alternate reality, to protect you and make sure you and Raptor Squadron played your part in the defeat of the Nexus forces."

Cassian's curiosity burned. "Sent by whom?"

Vigil shook his head. "That doesn't matter. Your reality is safe now. You'll never have to hear from us again."

"It matters to *me*!" Cassian replied, his voice rising, a surge of frustration building.

Vigil placed a reassuring hand on Cassian's shoulder. "Take it easy, kid. You and your people are safe. The Empire was saved."

Cassian's voice softened, but his frustration remained. "I still feel like I have no idea what was really going on."

Vigil sighed, his gaze turning downward. "Alright, I'll tell you what I can. My past is much like yours up to a certain point. In my reality, Bringi also came after me from another reality. But I didn't have a 'Vigil' to watch out for me. She destroyed our Empire to get to me. Those of us left banded together and confronted her on that station in the nebula. We barely managed to overwhelm her, but before we could end it, she escaped by jumping into another reality. We used the technology she left behind, combined with what we found on that station, to send me after her."

Cassian's mind raced to absorb this new information. "What's to stop her—or another version of her—from coming back?"

"She can't," Vigil assured him. "The station in the nebula was the key to traveling between realities. The one here no longer exists—I destroyed it."

Relief washed over Cassian. He had resigned himself to a life of looking over his shoulder, expecting that other, twisted Bringi to return. But Vigil's words offered him a rare sense of peace. Still, another thought surfaced.

"You said your time here is done. What does that mean?" Cassian asked.

Vigil hesitated, a brief silence passing between them. "It means I have to leave, Cassian. I have the ability to move between realities without the station now. My mission going forward is to ensure nothing like this ever happens again."

Cassian nodded, but curiosity got the better of him. "Any chance you can tell me what's ahead in my future?"

Vigil chuckled, a warmth in his scarred face that mirrored Cassian's own. "More battles, a wife who loves you, and children you'll adore."

Cassian raised an eyebrow, a smile tugging at his lips. "Children?"

Vigil's smile grew, but he said nothing more. "Goodbye, Cassian." With a nod, he placed his helmet back on, sealing it with a soft hiss, before turning to leave.

"Children," Cassian repeated to himself, feeling a surge of hope and excitement as he considered what his future might hold.

About the Author

Mixon Trammell is a career law enforcement officer in southwest Florida. He is currently serving as a school resource officer at a middle school. He enjoys training for strongman competitions and spending time with his beautiful wife and 4 children.